"The Guild
By Scott McGowan

©Scott McGowan 2016

This book is dedicated to all the steadfast ladies of *The Guild*. You are truly an inspiration and I would not be who I am today without the influence of my mother, grandmothers, aunts and great-aunts who have enjoyed being life-long members.

Chapter List

11	Chapter 1:	The News
14	Chapter 2:	The Bucket List
18	Chapter 3:	The Investigation
21	Chapter 4:	The Idea
24	Chapter 5:	The Guild
28	Chapter 6:	The Pamphlets
32	Chapter 7:	The Confession
35	Chapter 8:	The Shopping List
39	Chapter 9:	The Day Trip
46	Chapter 10:	The Lockup
50	Chapter 11:	The First Lesson
57	Chapter 12:	The Hangover
61	Chapter 13:	The Racetrack
69	Chapter 14:	The First Car
73	Chapter 15:	The Recovery
77	Chapter 16:	The Stubborn Woman
81	Chapter 17:	The Next Three Cars
87	Chapter 18:	The Final Lessons
91	Chapter 19:	The Confrontation
94	Chapter 20:	The New Doctor
97	Chapter 21:	The Hard Work
101	Chapter 22:	The New Diet
106	Chapter 23:	The Ten-year Itch
110	Chapter 24:	The Woman in Red

117	Chapter 25:	The Jail
121	Chapter 26:	The Backstory
125	Chapter 27:	The Irish
131	Chapter 28:	The Diagnostician
137	Chapter 29:	The Teasing
141	Chapter 30:	The Headmaster
146	Chapter 31:	The Check-up
150	Chapter 32:	The Lost Sheep
156	Chapter 33:	The Congratulatory Dinner
161	Chapter 34:	The Spit and Polish
166	Chapter 35:	The Weigh-in
171	Chapter 36:	The Morning Of
176	Chapter 37:	The Entrance
180	Chapter 38:	The Race Begins
181	Chapter 39:	The Race
190	Chapter 40:	The Finish Line
191	Chapter 41:	The Celebrations
194	Chapter 42:	The Broken Cup

"Keep alert, stand firm in your faith, be courageous, be strong. Let all that you do be done in love."

I Corinthians 16: 13-14

Chapter 1: The News

The clock chimed three o'clock when Agnus came through the front door of her house. Whilst slipping her handbag under her armpit, she slowly pulled off her overcoat and, her mind elsewhere, reached up without looking to hang it on the stand. She missed. As she let go, the overcoat slid down and landed on the floor behind her as she carried on oblivious.

Via the sittingroom which was pristine, she made her way directly to the kitchen where she discarded her handbag on the table and collapsed into a chair. She sat there a while, staring at nothing, her mind feeling cloudy and numb.

When she had gone down to the surgery that afternoon, she had not expected the outcome to be so conclusive. It was true, she knew that she had not been feeling herself lately but Agnus had put it down to getting older and hadn't really given it much notice. When the doctor had said that he wanted to put her in for the night for some tests, she questioned the need but went along with it to keep him happy. It was more than a bit of a shock when the results came back positive for Lewy Body Dementia.

Being a strong-minded Glaswegian woman in her mid-fifties, she hardly believed that it was true. Of course, she had found herself pouring the kettle into the tea jar once or twice and maybe she had even, *very occasionally*, dipped her morning toast in her tea[1] but they were things that a lot of people caught themselves doing and it didn't mean a thing.

The doctor had been adamant, however, explaining that things would get worse for her from here-on-in. She would start forgetting things and drift off every so often into a drowsy state; she would quickly become slower in everything she did

---

[1] Which she found she actually liked.

and her body would become hunched and stiff, giving the same effects as arthritis would; and more worryingly, hallucinations were also a possibility. All in all, things were not looking good for her future state of mind and the thought of it all was bearing down on top of her. Agnus continued to stare into space for a while, letting everything sink in. As she did, her eye was brought to a magazine which was sitting on the table.

I should say at this point that Agnus was a family woman. She had a loving husband and a good boy for a son. Her husband, Charlie, was a third generation factory worker. He had worked for many years at the old Ravenscraig estate until they finally closed the last of its operations. Since then, he had found work where he could; working whatever hours were required to keep his family in a comfortable state. Charlie worked hard and was often very tired because of it but he was the happiest man in the world because he had his family around him. He wanted nothing else.

Their son, Liam, was a bright boy. He had a keen interest in all things electrical and mechanical and was always stripping down the television, radio or whatever else he could find to see what made it tick. Charlie had recently instilled in him an interest in cars which he was a dab hand at himself and they found a passion that the two of them could share. Agnus loved to watch the pair of them, covered in oil, as they buried their heads in an engine.

Liam wasn't Charlie's real son, of course, but Charlie always loved him as such. It was nice for Agnus to see them bond like they did.

Charlie and Agnus had been married for ten years now with three years of courting before that and so Liam had grown fond of Charlie, accepting him as a parental figure. Things had gone so well for them, *until now*, and she had been happier than she could ever have hoped for.

Agnus kept staring at the magazine. It was one of Liam's and was all about racing cars. Liam and Charlie were currently building a car together, from scratch, and were aiming to have it ready in time to race in the annual rally, held each year near the top of Loch Lomond. There was a picture of a multi-coloured Ford, going at break-neck speeds down a muddy track. Agnus wasn't very keen on letting her seventeen-year-old son take part in such a dangerous sport but it was a dream that he needed to fulfil so she had put her fears aside. She did, however, speak to Charlie in private, saying that if anything were to happen to her wee lamb then *he* would be the one who would be requiring an ambulance.

Agnus got up, still in a state of detachment and put the kettle on. She slowly made herself a cup of tea in her favourite green mug, procured a crème de crème from the biscuit tin and took herself to bed, setting her alarm. As she lay there, the remains of her green mug of tea sitting on the side table getting cold, the words of her doctor kept running through her mind. As she drifted off, overwhelmed by the day's event, she wondered how she was ever going to cope.

Chapter 2: The Bucket List

Agnus woke slowly the next morning. It was a while before she realised that her alarm hadn't gone off. She wondered why for about a second before brushing it from her mind.

She had spoken with Charlie the previous night when he had returned from work and felt slightly better for it. Charlie had phoned the factory right there and then, telling them, in no uncertain terms that he would not be available the following day. Judging by the note on the bed, he was currently out at the chemist's collecting her prescriptions, of which there were many. He really was a wonderful and devoted husband. Agnus loved him dearly and was saddened at the strains he was going to have to endure as her mind and body began to fail, piece by piece.

Forcing herself out of bed, Agnus slipped on her dressing-gown and, taking her green mug with her, she made her way down to the kitchen. The house was empty. Liam must have found his way to school. He was a good boy, like that. When reaching the kitchen, Agnus washed the mug but as she reached over to put it on the rack to dry, it slipped out of her hand and hit the floor with a smash. Agnus stood there staring at the mess for a while before snapping herself out of it, saying to herself, "*Aggie, you silly girl, getting a fright from that. Behave!*"

Agnus cleaned up the broken mug and threw the remains into the bin and because they were needing to be done, she kept going and washed every other dish in sight. She then dried them all with a clean dishcloth and put them away neatly in their rightful place. While she was up and moving, she took the opportunity to dust down the sides. In order to do that, she first had to clear them of all the clutter.

The clutter being cleared and the sides dusted down, Agnus felt that she really should give the cupboards a long-due clean and so proceeded to empty them all onto the kitchen table, dusting each item as she went. A hot soapy sponge later and a lot of elbow grease, she had the cupboards shining like they were new. Taking the opportunity, as everything was collated on the table, she decided to rearrange where everything went. This took her a little time but she completed her task successfully before standing up straight in the middle of the room, glaring at the result with her arms crossed and exhaled.

Agnus started breathing again. Her body relaxed and her face did the same. The glare became that of surrender and dejection.

It was at this moment when the infuriating whistle of the boiling kettle pierced her hearing and Agnus was brought back to reality. She made her way over to the stove and lifted the kettle off the electric hob, by use of the previously mentioned dishcloth.

Making herself a cup of tea, she was still in a daze. It was a hard thing to come to terms with. To wrap your head around the fact that you're slowly going to break down from the inside is no easy thing and Agnus felt like it was all a dream. Even now, as she sat at the kitchen table, she had the strangest feeling that nothing was real except her. Her mind had a certain numbness to it as well. Ever since she found out the test results, she was finding it hard to think, like a cloud was engulfing her brain.

For the first time in years, as Agnus sat there, depressed and forlorn, she started to think about all the things she had wanted to do in her life. She'd never had any such a thing as a 'bucket list', growing up. That was more a younger generation's thing. When she was younger, though, Agnus had climbed mountains and trekked numerous Scottish trails which had tested many a man and now that she was older, she wanted to experience some new type of thrill.

Bungee Jumping was a straight no-no. There was no way she was going to jump off some bridge with nothing but a giant elastic band tied to her ankles. She had seen people do it on the television and it had always looked like a damn silly thing to do. If the band snapped, which they were always adamant that it wouldn't, then she would be in a bit of a stick and cut her life a lot shorter than it was already. That was not her plan.

Skydiving was more of the same. Agnus was quite sure that she wasn't willing to jump out of a perfectly good plane. If it was on fire… then fair enough, she might take the plunge but they weren't likely to start an electrical fire in the cockpit just to make her happy.

The radio which was on the counter was playing a pleasant tune, *"Express Yourself"*, by the notorious and often misrepresented rap group N.W.A. She thought about her problem some more, still feeling numb all over and the song lyrics rolling through her head.

#"There's no fessin' and guessin' while I'm expressin myself. It's crazy to see people be what society wants them to be. But not me!"

Her eyes were drawn, once again, to the magazine that sat on the table. Racing cars. Maybe… *no*. It was certainly exciting and there was no way that Charlie and Liam could protest, them having entered the thing themselves but… no, she couldn't. Agnus knew next to nothing about cars. She supposed that she could always learn but would there be time before the competition started? She looked again at the magazine. She supposed that it wouldn't do any harm to look into it, you know, just out of interest. It wasn't like she was actually going to go through with it.

With a one-nostril sniff, Agnus picked up the magazine and started to read.

Chapter 3: The Investigation

Agnus was still reading the magazine when Charlie came back from the shops. He came straight through to the kitchen and carefully laid his overflowing carrier bags on the other end of the table from where Agnus was seated. He then sat down himself next to her and asked how she was holding up.

"Well," replied Agnus, "I wasn't feeling too bright earlier. I even went on a cleaning binge."

"I can see that," said Charlie, looking around and smiling softly. "The place looks brand new. It really sparkles."

Agnus smiled. "Well," she said, "I'm feeling a bit better in myself now."

"I'm glad," Charlie replied. "Now, I got you a few things while I was out."

Charlie dragged his two bags across the table to him and proceeded to present each item, one by one. There were her medications from the chemist, of course. They came in different shapes and colours and each had a different logo stamped on them.

Charlie also pulled out of his bags, six tins of chicken soup; three tubs of chocolate fudge ice cream with tiny bits of vanilla fudge mixed through it; the latest Cosmopolitan, with bright smiling women on the front cover; two bags of butterbeans which were nothing special but just happened to be her favourite; and a box of tissues.

"I've also got the Chinese on speed dial," Charlie concluded, "if you're up for something proper to eat."

Agnus smiled at this and said that she would be fine enough with just the soup. It was all she felt like having anyway. She wasn't all that hungry for food at the moment. Brushing her troubles off, for a moment, Agnus held up the racing magazine.

"I've just been looking through this," she said. "It seems very interesting."

"It's a guy thing, love," said Charlie, apologising on behalf of his entire gender.

"Do you think you've got a chance of winning?" Agnus asked.

"We hope so. We've been working very hard to get the car up to a decent standard."

"So you can't just enter any car into the race, then?" probed Agnus.

"Oh no," replied Charlie. "There are very specific guidelines to what you can put in your car. There's the safety aspects as well as allowing fair competition."

"Really? I take it you have a copy of these requirements?" Agnus enquired further.

"Yes," Charlie confirmed, "everyone gets a copy when they register. If any entrant fails to have their car ready by midday on the eve of the race, then they will be instantly disqualified."

"Hmmm," mumbled Agnus.

"You seem to be taking a keen interest in this all of a sudden," said Charlie, curiously.

"Just inquisitive about what my boys are up to," replied Agnus, snapping out of her inklings and putting the magazine on the side behind her, out of sight. "Speaking of which, it's near four-thirty and Liam's not back yet."

"He's stopping off to get some wiring from my mate, Sparky. He'll be back by half-five."

"Who's Sparky, when he's at home?" Agnus asked, concerned.

"Me and Sparky have been friends since school. He's been out working in Spain for gone seventeen years, now. He's a good guy and Liam's met him before, so don't worry."

Agnus relaxed, realizing that she was probably fretting over nothing.

"Are you really doing alright?" asked Charlie, honest concern in his voice.

"I am," Agnus replied, smiling, "but I am feeling a bit tired. I think I'm going to have myself a bath and a sleep. I'm sure I'll be feeling better by tomorrow."

Charlie smiled, sadly and patted her hand. "I'm sure you will," he said. "You sit here, I'll run the bath."

As she lovingly watched him leave the room, Agnus smiled properly for the first time since hearing the news. Charlie was a wonderful man and she was lucky to have him.

Chapter 4: The Idea

Agnus lay in the bath, surrounded by a mass of bubbles which smelled very strongly of lavender. Charlie must have done his research because she was more relaxed than she had been since before the doctor's. There were candles lain around the room as well. They were all different colours and smells. Charlie must have been unable to decide upon one and just taken the lot. Agnus smiled. She could really imagine him fussing around in the shop with a concentrated look on his face as he tried to get his self-appointed task correct. He'd even come running in again, just as she was about to dip her toe in, with an incense stick as a hurried afterthought.

She closed her eyes. In a state of pure Zen, her mind was drawn back to what she had been reading in her son's magazine. It did intrigue her. The thought of having one last experience of excitement before the dementia started to take over was uplifting and she was really starting to come around to the idea. She did wonder, however, how she would do it. She was not trained in any form of mechanics and she presumed that it wasn't something you could just pick up quickly. If she did go ahead with it, this would not be a *me, myself and I* situation. She would need some help.

Thinking about this some more as she lay in her hot bath, she warmed to the idea and decided to look into it a bit more. However, it could wait until after her soak and a good night's rest.

✧

The next day Agnus awoke with a bit more energy than she had done the day before. The idea had festered and, although the depression still lingered, she felt that, if she really decided to proceed, there was an element of hope. This spurred her on, giving her a wee boost for the day.

In the evening, she would have her weekly Guild night at the church. It was a good way to keep up with people and have a well-needed gossip. Agnus had decided, before going to sleep, that she would put her idea to her three friends at the Guild. Maybe they could give her some idea of how to go forward. Wasn't Lilly's husband working in a garage at the moment? That could help. He would certainly know what bits went where.

Agnus decided to put the thought aside, for now. There were daytime things that needed to be done and she was going to treat today just like any other. She went through to the sittingroom with a carrier bag and started collecting anything that was waste. She then took the bag through to the kitchen to put it in the bin. The bin was full so she pulled the white bag out and placed the carrier inside before tying it up and depositing the lot in the green bin outside. As it happened, it was bin night so Agnus wheeled the green bin around to the front of the house and left it sitting on the pavement.

Back in the sittingroom, Agnus took her duster out and a can of Pledge spray polish and went around each unit in turn. This done, she located Henry in Liam's room. Why he was there was a mystery. He certainly hadn't been used. Agnus took Henry downstairs and hoovered all the carpeting before proceeding onto the stairwell and finishing off with the upstairs. She put Henry back into the cupboard under the stairs where he belonged, locking the door with the small key that permanently sat in the lock.

Agnus went on like this with her new-found energy all day and had only just completed her final task[2] at four o'clock when Charlie returned for the day.

Agnus and Charlie sat at the kitchen table, waiting Liam's return from school, sipping cups of tea and talking about nothing in particular. It was just nice to be in each other's company.

✷

When Liam got home, he was sent up to clear his floor of all but furniture. He was back down in less than thirty minutes so Agnus deduced that his wardrobe would now need a good going over.

The three of them had dinner and afterwards, Charlie and Liam insisted on doing the washing up. Agnus was happy about this as it gave her a little time before heading out to the Guild to think about what she was actually going to say to the girls when she saw them that evening. She wasn't sure how they were going to take her madcap idea. Would they laugh it off? Would they think her crazy? Would they call the hospital and tell them that her dementia had progressed quicker than expected?

She hoped they would understand her need to have one last bit of fun before, well, *you know*. Her group of friends were limited and so if they were not willing to help her then she was unlikely to take her idea much further. As she thought, she slipped off to sleep and was only woken again, slightly refreshed, a half-hour before she was due to leave for the Guild.

---

[2] Lamb shank in the oven with new potatoes and carrots on the boil.

Chapter 5: The Guild

Agnus stepped out of the faded blue Ford Fiesta and waved goodbye to Charlie as he drove off again. She turned and looked up at the Church. The building itself was around one hundred and fifty years old and had stood the test of time. There were a few patches, here and there but generally, the building was as good now as it was when it was built. The place had survived the blitz relatively unharmed as well as many other skirmishes over the years. The only thing that concerned her was when they installed a metal conductor on the roof to catch lightning strikes. This seemed like a lack of faith, in her humble opinion. It was His house, after all. If He wanted to burn it down, let Him. *Gods will be done.*

She took a breath and walked up the steps to the big hall where the meeting would take place. As she got to the top of the steps, she was met by an elderly lady with wavy white hair and a stern but happy look about her. She wore a green tweed jacket and heavy green trousers to match. Her name was Eva Harris and she had moved down to Glasgow, from the Hebridean Islands, a few years previously. Agnus and Eva had soon hit it off and came to be close friends.

"Agnus, love," Eva greeted when she saw her friend climbing the final few steps, "how are you doing? Did you get your results back, the other day?"

Agnus sighed. "I did," she replied. "We'll talk about it later. Let's get in out of the cold for now."

Eva was curious but nodded amiably and followed Agnus in and through to the big hall. When they got there, there were many other women and even a couple of men. This had not always been the case. It wasn't until quite recently that the *Women's Guild* had moved with the times and become simply *The Guild*, allowing men into its order.

As she looked over the swarm of members, Agnus saw her other two friends, sitting at a table on the other side of the room. She tapped Eva on the arm to indicate that she had found their quarry and moved across the hall to see them.

The two ladies who sat there were dissimilar in every way. Being mother and daughter wasn't much help. The mother, *Big May*, was as tough as old boots. She had worked in the steel factories all her days and had developed a rough demeanour. Big May was the nicest person around but the way she put things when she spoke and her radical honesty only made to make some people shy away.

The daughter, Lilly, was a different kettle of fish. As Agnus and Eva approached, they could see the skinny girl clearly doing some crochet under the table, so as not to draw the attention of her mother. Big May saw this kind of thing frivolous and not really worth one's time but Lilly was such a quiet soul. She enjoyed chatting with her friends but did tend to stumble over her words when she was nervous or unsure of something. She seemed to be nervous quite a lot.

"Agnus, Eva, how are you both?" greeted Big May as they all gathered around the table.

"I'm fine," said Eva, "but Agnus is being all mysterious."

"How did you get on with the doctor's the other day? I know you were there. Sheena's aunt Bessie's daughter-in-law was in there getting her Bobby's ears dewaxed and said that she saw you going into Doctor Cameron's office."

Agnus hoped that the girl hadn't seen her coming back out again. She must have looked a right state. "I wanted to speak to you all together before I said anything," she replied to Eva's well-meant scorn.

"Well, come on dear," said Big May. "You've got us on tender hooks, here."

She decided to just give it to them straight. "It's Lewy Body," she said, simply.

The table went quiet as the information sunk in.

"I'm so sorry, love," said Eva, eventually. "I had no idea."

"Neither did I," Agnus replied. "I wasn't expecting the tests to show anything at all. Really didn't think there was anything of much wrong with me, to tell you the truth," She sighed. "Just shows how wrong you can be."

"Is there anything we can do to help?" asked Big May.

Agnus looked up with a cheeky grin. "Well," she said, "It's funny you should say that because there is something I want to do before… well, *you know*."

"Anything you want to do, dear," said Big May, "just say it and it's done."

"Well," she said…

※

"You can't be serious," said Eva when Agnus had finished her tale.

"Let me get this straight," Big May jumped in. "You want to build a fully functioning rally car and race it in that blasted competition your husband and son have put themselves into?"

"But we don't know anything about cars," said Lilly.

"No," replied Agnus, "but your husband does."

"Yes," Lilly conceded, "but this sounds like a lot of work and he's very busy. I don't think he'd be able to help that much."

"He'd do it for you," argued Big May, sternly.

"Aww, Mum," replied Lilly, "don't you go putting pressure on him. He's a good man and he works hard to keep us afloat."

"If you love someone, you do anything in your power to help them and, *dear*, this would really help us… I mean you," she quickly corrected.

"But mum," sighed Lilly.

"But me no buts," Big May replied and, addressing Agnus, she continued, saying, "I'm sure he'll come around."

Agnus smiled a soft smile. "I'm so glad to have friends like you."

Chapter 6: The Pamphlets

When Agnus awoke, the morning after the Guild, she wasn't feeling too well in herself. The girls had all agreed to at least test out her plan which was a weight off her shoulders but, with the strain of the last few days and keeping herself busy through it, she was starting to get a migraine right behind the eyes. Agnus put it down to overstaining herself and decided to make the day her own.

She made herself some herbal tea and fished out the box of Tunnock's tea cakes from her hiding place before sitting down in her comfy armchair in front of the television. As it happened, her favourite show, 'The Chase', was on. It was a repeat from the night before but as she was so busy, she had failed to see it. She had time to catch up now, though.

Somebody must have made an accidental blue joke because at present, the host, Bradley, was in a state of the giggles. To be more precise he was in a state of *endeavouring not to let the giggles out*. His mouth was shut tightly, his lips curling over his teeth, and he had a huge pained grin on his face which was starting to turn red with the strain of trying not to burst out laughing on national television. According to the subtitles which were unusual on this show, Bradley had been in this state for seven minutes and forty-seven seconds. He was going for a new record.

As she sipped her tea, wincing at the pain of her migraine, Agnus opened her handbag and pulled out some information pamphlets which she had received from Doctor Cameron. The first one described the symptoms which she wouldn't readily forget after the Doctor's telling. The one that concerned her the most was the possibility of hallucinations. She didn't like the idea of that. She couldn't think of anything worse than not knowing her own mind. She wondered when they would start.

A sharp hot pain ran straight through her head.

"Pretty soon, I'd expect," said an unfamiliar voice.

Agnus looked over quickly to where the voice had come from and saw with great shock, two men sitting uncomfortably on her couch. The first one who sat closest to Agnus was dressed in a white suit which was odd in itself and had a nervous smile on his face. The second man, who didn't seem to want to be there either, wore a pair of old (black denim) trousers; black 'AC\DC' t-shirt; and a soft black leather jacket. They did not look at ease on Agnus' flowery settee.

Agnus opened her mouth to speak but, in her state of shock, no words came out.

After a couple of seconds of opening and closing her mouth, she managed to cough up the words, "Who are you and what the blazes are you doing in my house?"

"Madam!" the man in white groaned at the sound of the expletive.

"That's what I'm talking about," smiled the man in black.

"Don't you *Madam* me," said Agnus, finding her will again. "Who are you?"

"Well," said the man in black, sharing a look with the man in white, "you know they say that everyone has an Angel on one shoulder and a Daemon on the other?"

"Yes," replied Agnus, getting worried.

"Well, we're yours," he concluded. "My name is Sergey and this here is Tarquin."

"You're an Angel and a Daemon?" Agnus asked, not believing a single word of it.

"To be more precise, we are the two opposing halves of your own mind. We are not what you would call real, per say."

"So, which one of you is which?" Agnus asked, sarcastically.

Sergey looked at Tarquin, eyebrow raised. "Is she serious?" he asked.

"Of course I'm not serious," snapped Agnus. She rubbed her forehead in exasperation. "So, what you're telling me is that you're both just figments of my imagination?"

"That's a very simplified expiation," replied Sergey, a little hurt.

"Be nice," said Tarquin, elbowing Sergey in the ribs. "This is a lot for her to deal with."

"I didn't come here to be called a figment of somebody's imagination," Sergey moaned.

"Why *are* you here?" asked Agnus, getting less scared and more annoyed at these two impossible gentlemen.

"Like he said," replied Tarquin, "we are the part of your mind that conflicts. My job is to keep you on a good path."

"And mine," Sergey piped in, "is to make sure you get to experience all that life has to offer."

"And what if those remits clash?" asked Agnus.

"Then," replied Sergey, "you'll have a decision to make."

Agnus thought on this. "Are you going to be following me around all the time, then?" she asked.

"I shouldn't think so," Tarquin replied. "We'll probably just pop in, every now and then."

"I can't believe this is happening," Agnus said, to herself. "I'm sitting in my own livingroom, talking to two imaginary gentlemen. This can't be a good sign."

Tarquin and Sergey sat there for another forty-five minutes as Agnus watched her game-show, attempting to ignore the fictional pair. This was hard because they kept arguing over the answers to the questions that Bradley was asking.

Eventually, Agnus had to split them up. *She* sat on the couch and sent each of the other two to a chair on opposing side of her. They sat in silence as Agnus continued watching her show and when she eventually looked up again they were both gone. Not only that, her migraine had cleared up, too.

Chapter 7: The Confession

That afternoon, Agnus went out to the garage where Charlie and Liam were working on their car. It did Agnus good to see them in their orange boiler suits, covered head to toe in thick oil and drilling away at something or another. She smiled as she entered and gave a call out to Charlie to get his attention. Charlie immediately shut off the drill and stood up.

"Hello, darling," he said. "Is everything alright? Nothing's happened has it?"

"No, no," said Agnus, quickly, "nothing's wrong. I've just got something to tell you both."

Charlie looked worried.

"Don't fret," Agnus comforted. "It's nothing bad."

"Well, what is it, then?" asked Liam. "Just tell us."

"Well," said Agnus, "since the other day, I've had a yearning for one last adventure before this thing takes over."

"That sounds fair enough," sad Charlie. "Why the ominous approach?"

"It's what I'm looking to do that might concern you," replied Agnus.

"And what would that be?" asked Charlie. "I do hope you're not going to try and climb Everest again. It didn't end up too well last time and that was fifteen years ago."

"That was when we first met," said Agnus, smiling softly.

"Exactly," smiled Charlie. "I'm not having you run off with some other hot bit of stuff you find up a mountain. *I'm not letting you out of my sight!*"

"That shouldn't be a problem," replied Agnus. "That's what I wanted to tell you. I've decided what I'm going to attempt."

"Which is?" asked Liam, very curious about what his madcap mother was about to do.

"I'm going to enter this race of yours," Agnus answered.

The two boys went silent for a second or three as the information sunk in. Then, both at once, they burst out laughing.

Agnus stood there in her pinny, fists on her hips and her jaw sticking out, and glared at the two dead men. "Is there a problem, here?" she asked, firmly.

Charlie quickly tried to stop the giggles, saying, "Sorry love. No offence meant but you know nothing about the insides of a car. It's not a one-man job anyway… or a one-woman job as the case may be."

"I've got help," said Agnus, indignantly. "I'm not that daft, yet."

"Aggie, I didn't mean that," said Charlie, hurriedly.

"I know," said Agnus. "The girls are going to help me and young Lilly's husband is a mechanic so he's going to look after us. *Even if he doesn't know it yet*," she added in her head.

It sounds like you've made a good start," said Charlie. "I say go for it. It'll be good for you to have a project."

After a quick chat with the boys about the regulations and when the car had to be ready by, Agnus went back into the house to make dinner. As she did, she thought hard about how they should proceed. They should really find a car, for starters. She'd speak to Lilly's husband about that. He'd know where to find an old car that would suit the purpose.

Yes, everything was looking more possible. This might actually work.

For the rest of the afternoon, Agnus sat in her chair watching old racing videos that Liam had lent her. She listened to the squeal of the breaks as the cars went speeding around the dirt tracks, she saw with little surprise when they skidded out of control and she felt it every time one of them took a corner too fast and ended up wedged in a tree.

Tarquin and Sergey failed to show their faces for the rest of the day, too which was a relief, and Agnus really did feel better. She had something to aim for… something to hope for. That, she felt was the key to getting through this illness which had been flung upon her. She needed some kind of hope and this new project of hers, whether they managed to pull it off or not, would do very well indeed. She was starting to get chills of excitement at the thought of it all.

Chapter 8: The Shopping List

In the evening, the ladies arrived. The four of them sat around the kitchen table which held a silver tea-tray with a pot and four mugs. There was also a small jug of milk, a bowl of sugar and a plate of cakes and biscuits.

Agnus looked around at her three friends who sat there with their small pads and pencils in front of them. It was encouraging that they were all serious about helping her do this. If she were being honest with herself, it was a silly undertaking and a dangerous one at that. She remembered some of the accidents she had seen on Liam's videos and wondered, not for the last time, if whoever drove the thing wouldn't end up going out the same way. *That might not be such a bad thing if it were me*, she thought. Go out in one quick blaze of glory. Better that than what she was going to have to go through.

"That's it, my girl," came the loathsome voice of Sergey. "Hell, Leather and all that jazz."

Agnus looked over to the irritant, then back to her friends before bringing her gaze back to Sergey again.

"Don't worry," said Tarquin, "they can't see us. All in your head, remember?"

Agnus looked back to her friends who were talking amongst themselves.

"*Well, if this is all in my head,*" Agnus thought, "*then you know what I'm thinking.*"

"Indeed we do," replied Sergey, "and, well I never, that thought you just had of me was quite graphic. I think I might be offended. I'm only here to help, you know."

"*Yeah, right,*" Agnus thought, "*Only my best interests at heart eh?*"

"Here," continued Sergey, unabashed, "I want you to have that *blaze of glory*. I think it would be horrible to linger, unable to know what's real and what's not; your body wasting away."

"Don't you listen to him," Tarquin piped in. "That's no way to deal with this. This is a good project you've got here. See it through and do it right. There is still hope."

"*This is one of those decisions you were talking about, isn't it,*" Agnus thought, accusingly.

The two just stared at her, silently.

Agnus decided.

She looked up at her friends. "Ladies," she said, "shall we begin?"

☆

As they discussed matters, the ladies passed the magazine around.

"So, you want us to build one of these things?" asked Eva. "We can't just buy one pre-made?"

"I don't think that's really in the spirit of the thing," Agnus replied.

"What type of cars are popular, then?" asked Big May.

"Subaru seem to be quite common and there's always the Ford," replied Agnus.

"I like the white..." Lilly started to say, "*what was it?*" She grabbed the magazine from her mother and flicked through until she found the page she was looking for. "Here we go. It's called the Lancia... *Delta.*"

"And where are we going to find one of those?" asked Big May, irritably. "We should keep things as simple as possible. The Fords are generally very widespread. We should go for one of those. Either that or the Subaru, if we come across one."

Agnus looked over to Lilly, "I'm sorry Lilly but I think she might be right. It's going to be hard enough to find a suitable car without limiting ourselves to something that may not even be out there."

Lilly nodded slowly if reluctantly.

"Anyway," said Eva, "isn't this something we should be talking to your husband about?"

"Tommy's on his way," replied Lilly. "He should be here shortly."

"It'll be nice to have someone who can help us through this," said Agnus.

"It took a bit of persuasion," Lilly replied. "He wasn't very chuffed at losing his evenings in order to hang out with… *how did he put it?...* oh yes, '*A bunch o' wumen!*'"

"We'll soon have him in shape," said Big May. "He'll be happy as chips once he gets his head into that engine."

"Quite right," Eva agreed. "He'll cope."

Agnus thought that Big May was mixing up her metaphors but hoped that Tommy would look kindly on the four friends. She really wanted this to work.

✧

Tommy eventually made an appearance and threw himself down onto a chair, saying, "Right ladies. If we're going to do this it's going to be a lot of work and even then we may not complete it in time for the race."

"I'm sure, with your help, we'll manage it," said Agnus, smiling.

"Yeah, well we'll see," Tommy replied, "but there's one thing I'm going to need before we go any further."

"What?" asked the four women in unison.

"A mug of tea," Tommy answered.

A mug of warm tea was duly made and ushered over to him. He sat there for a minute, inhaling the warmth from his mug and breathing slowly in and out. As Agnus was about to say something, Tommy looked over to her, saying, "Ok. First of all, what is it you really want to accomplish here?"

"Well," said Agnus, slowly, "we want to build a car and race it in the Loch Lomond Rally."

"Right," said Tommy, "so winning the thing isn't your biggest concern?"

"No," replied Agnus. "Just being able to race is enough. If we win, then all the better but it's not the be all and end all."

"That's some good news," Tommy continued. "It's going to be hard enough to get a suitable car to regulation standards without the added pressure of making it a contender for the cup."

The ladies all agreed that getting their car into the race was their main objective and so they started to plan out all the things they would need to do in order to make this all work. Tommy said that he would handle the regulators and entry officials and even get them a suitable car. It would be the ladies' job to locate and purchase all the tools and equipment they would need. Tommy would obviously write down what it was they were looking for but it was down to them to seek and find. Tommy had a day-job after all and wasn't able to run around the town looking for car parts.

This being agreed, they made a list. The ladies came to referring to it as their, *'Shopping List'* which made even Tommy let out a short smile.

Chapter 9: The Day Trip

Agnus met the ladies at the bus stop on Douglas Street at twenty past six in the morning. With Tommy's help, they had eventually made a long list of all the equipment they were going to need. There was no mistake, this was going to be an expensive trip but Agnus had done well in her career life over the years and had enough savings to be able to afford all the things they were going to have to buy.

Because there were so many items on their shopping list, they were not going to be getting the bus into town. Instead, they would jump on the 204 until they got near to Tommy's garage. From there, they would borrow a nondescript white panel van and drive it to the Great Western Road where lay the Machine Mart. It was there that they would be able to find at least most of what they required.

As Agnus turned the corner onto Douglas Street, she saw her three friends waiting patiently under the shelter. Big May and Eva were sitting on the thin strip of plastic covered metal which the bus companies had decided was the best seating they could provide. Lilly had chosen to protect her posterior, what there was of it, and so stood just under the shelter, holding her cloth bag in front of her with both hands.

Agnus strolled up to them, giving the usual greetings, and sat down next to Big May. "I'm starting to get a bit excited," she said.

Big May and Eva who had been more than a little overwhelmed by Tommy's words the previous night, looked at each other before saying, in unison, "Aye, right."

Lilly had been party to a conversation between the two elder ladies when they had eventually left Agnus' house, the night before, where they had expressed concern for this dubious undertaking. "I think what they mean," Lilly said to Agnus, "is that this is becoming very real, very fast, and we're all finding it a little daunting. Not that we don't want to keep going," she continued quickly, "just that it may take us a wee bit to get our heads around all of this."

"I think that's the most I've ever heard you say, in one go," said Agnus, smiling, "but seriously, I know what you're saying. It's a lot to take in, I'm sure, but we can do this and I want it to be done by *us*. I wouldn't feel right doing it with anyone else."

"Like she said," replied Big May, "we're not backing out, just a little overawed with what we're going to have to do, in order to build this car and race it. It is a large job and there's no guarantee that we'll even finish the car in time for this viewing that's going to happen before the start of it all."

"I know and I understand. We'll take everything as it comes and if anyone has any problems or questions we'll make sure that they're not ignored."

"Sounds fair," said Eva.

They came to this conclusion just in time. As Eva's words left her lips, the single-decker came wobbling around the corner. Agnus wondered why, with all the technology they had these days, they couldn't fit a bus with the proper suspension.

"It's the cheap fixings," came an unwanted voice as Agnus followed her three friends onto the bus.

"*What are you two doing here?*" she thought, angrily, in Sergey's direction. He was holding a cigarette between his lips and patting all his pockets, in search for a match.

"That's nice, isn't it," cowed Sergey, his unlit fag flapping up and down as he spoke. "We pop in for a nice wee chat and all we get is abuse."

"*I don't have time for this,*" Agnus thought.

"You could have plenty time for a lot of things if you stop all this car nonsense," replied Sergey.

"*It's not nonsense,*" Agnus thought, strongly.

"Quite right," said Tarquin, who had popped up on the other side of Agnus. "This is good for you. It's a new challenge to overcome. '*There are no problems, only opportunities to be creative.*' Dorye Roettger said that."

"The girls don't seem to think so," replied Sergey. "They're not sure about this at all."

"*That's true,*" Agnus thought, "*They would all quit today if I wasn't ill.*"

"Exactly," said Sergey, who had finally found a match and was puffing away.

Agnus scowled at the Daemon, showed her pass to the bus driver and followed her friends to the middle of the aisle.

"They want to help," said Tarquin as he sat beside Sergey in the seats directly behind Agnus.

"That may be," snorted Sergey, "but, trust me, tensions will rise and you'll all end up biting each other's heads off. It's not worth the trouble."

"Don't you listen to him," Tarquin said, softly as he patted Agnus on the shoulder. "You're all good friends and whatever happens you'll be able to deal with it. Anyway, they wouldn't stop now even if you told them to."

"*I guess you're right,*" thought Agnus, as she half listened to the ladies gossip about '…him around the corner from Jeanie's cousin Fred…'. "*I'll just have to keep an eye on everyone. Fix any problems when they pop up.*"

"Good choice," Tarquin smiled as he licked the tip of his index finger and drew an imaginary '1' in front of Sergey's face.

"Whatever," hawed Sergey. "I'm outta here," and, with that, he vanished.

"Good luck," Tarquin whispered, conspiratorially, before popping out of existence himself.

The two annoyances gone, Agnus relaxed. "Peace at last," she thought, before putting her mind to the task in hand.

✽

As the bus drove from stop to stop, across the town, the girls went through the list again. There were a few items on there that were obvious, like tool kits and jacks but there were a great deal more items that they had never conceived of using. Some they had never even heard of.

"What's a *'multimeter'?*" asked Eva.

"I'm not sure," replied Agnus. "Maybe it's like one of those meter stick we had at school… only longer."

"It's a voltage tester," said Lilly, casually flicking through one of her husband's car magazines. "It's to make sure your electrics are all running the right power etcetera."

"Where did that come from?" asked Big May.

"Oh," Lilly replied, looking up from her read, "I'm forever pulling Tommy's out from the back of the couch."

"Wait a minute," said Eva, "are you trying to tell us that you know about all this stuff?"

"Bits and pieces," Lilly confessed, coolly. "I suppose I've picked up a few things over the years. Tommy used to take me into the garage, at night, when we were first courting."

"Did he now?" huffed Big May.

"Not like that," Lilly sighed, "he would open up a car and tell me what all the bits did."

"Very romantic," Big May scorned.

"It was nice," Lilly replied, shyly.

"Right then, it's decided," said Agnus, "you're in charge of making sure we don't get robbed by these merchants today."

After some hesitation from the nervous girl, the discussion was concluded and Lilly was voted in, three-to-one. The fact that Lilly seemed to understand what was going on made Agnus and the other two ladies feel a bit surer about the day and this gave them all a lift. Smiles came out, even though it was still early in the morning, and the world seemed shiny again.

✻

They picked up the van from the garage, Big May walking around it and kicking the tires; and Lilly taking studious notes, regarding any scratches already present. From there, they drove out to the Machine Mart and parked in a spot, ten feet from the entrance.

"Ok, ladies," said Agnus, "Lilly here will speak to the boy regarding the list. We'll follow them around collecting everything into the trollies."

"Some of the things are pretty big and heavy," said Lilly.

"That's fine," replied Eva with a naughty grin, "I'm sure they'll be *delighted* to load them into the van for us."

"I'm sure," said Lilly, who clearly wasn't. "Just let me do the talking."

"Hey," Big May replied, holding up her hands up, "We're good. This *is* all your area of expertise, after all."

The ladies, the three elders grabbing a trolley each as they did, entered the Machine Mart and surveyed the terrain. Everywhere they looked was filled with shelves, crammed with tools of every kind. There were many machines of unknown description on display with men in red sweaters, directed by other men in white shirts, demonstrating the power of the aforesaid machines. Some were for cutting, others were for welding and still others were for the firing of various objects, be they nail, chipping or cladding.

Lilly tried to grab the attention of a red-sweatered boy as he scurried past her but to no avail. He was gone just as quickly as he had appeared. She tried another couple of times but the four ladies went completely un-noticed. Eventually, Eva reached out and grabbed one of the white-shirted gentlemen by the collar and pulled him up close to her face, saying, "Right, sonny boy, you just listen here. We are looking for everything on this list, here," she snapped her fingers quickly in the air and Lilly hurriedly passed her the list, "and we would be obliged if you could give us some assistance."

The man looked, cock-eyed at the piece of paper and weighed up his chances of making it to lunch without mishap. "Of course, I...I...ladies," he stammered, showing all his teeth in an attempt to appear willing, "anything I can do to alleviate your current predicaments."

"You're a fast learner," Eva replied, releasing the man. She handed him the list and told him where the van was. "We'll just have a look around while you find all that," she said to the man. "We'll be back shortly."

They left the shaking man who was patting around his pockets for his heart medication and went for a stroll around the store. As they went, Lilly explained what some of the things were for and took them over to the automotive section in order to give them a better idea of what kind of things they'd be working with.

Returning a couple of hours later, they came back to a trolley caravan lining the front of the store and out into the parking lot. They followed the line of trolleys and discovered that they led to the back of *their* van. The white shirted man was standing there getting more and more stressed. When he saw the ladies approaching, he jumped to attention, saying, "The key's madam, if you would be so kind, and we'll start loading everything in."

"Certainly, young man," replied Eva, with what she thought was a posh accent, handing him the keys to the van.

"Just make sure you don't scratch anything," shouted Lilly, as he turned his back on them.

With the four ladies breathing down their necks, the van was loaded, eventually (without a scratch) and the ladies drove off with their newly acquired load. Lilly waved pleasantly out of the window as they drove away, shouting, "Thank you very much. We'll definitely recommend you to all our friends."

Every man there winced at the thought of more women invading their sanctuary. It was not a nice thought and the experience of these ladies, just the once, was enough to last them a lifetime.

"So, what now?" asked Eva as they trundled along. "Where do you want me to drive this thing? Back to yours?"

"No," replied Agnus, "there's no space at mine for all this. Big May's got us a lockup down by the docks. We can make as much noise as we like and nobody will bother themselves about us."

"Sounds good," replied Eva. "You direct and I'll drive."

Chapter 10: The Lockup

Big May had looked at her watch, a mere three minutes after leaving the Machine Mart, and said, "That's it gone one o'clock. We should stop off somewhere and get ourselves an afternoon tea. I think we've earned it."

"Fair enough," answered Agnus, "but it'll have to be somewhere with adequate parking."

They found a place up a long lane which opened up a mile down the track to show a stately home style hotel.

"This'll do nicely," said Eva, as she swung the laden van around the carpark and into a space that Agnus had thought would be too tight.

"Doesn't it just fit like a glove," said Eva with a big smile.

The others said nothing but made their way quickly to the exit, getting down out of the van and onto firmer ground. They patted themselves down and fixed themselves before giving Eva a nasty look as they made their way into the hotel.

It was a nice and peaceful lunch; once Agnus, Big May and Lilly had gotten over Eva's driving. The afternoon tea provided was more than adequate and even surpassed their hopes. As they looked out of the wide windows of the lounge area, they could see a burn, untouched by man, slipping peacefully downstream. The birds were even out. Agnus felt very relaxed as she listened to their songs.

Before long, however, it was time to go and so they packaged what was left of the afternoon tea into some napkins before being transferred to a couple of handbags; paid their bill, leaving a substantial gratuity payment[3]; and went on their way,

---

[3] A tip.

making sure to tell Eva to keep the van below forty miles per hour.

After a half hour's journey, they finally arrived at the lockup where they were astounded to see five large gentlemen standing around the entrance.

"I was promised that we would not be bothered, down here," said Big May, angrily. "I'm going to have serious words with somebody as soon as we're out of here."

Agnus looked at Eva, noticing that she had a concentrated look on her face and that she was not slowing down. Agnus had the sudden thought that her friend was going to drive the van straight into them and she may well have done if Lilly hadn't shouted out in terror, "*Stop! I know them!*"

Eva suddenly slammed on the handbrake and spun the van into a one-hundred-and-eighty-degree turn, where she quickly knocked it into reverse and sped backwards, her head sticking out the window for a better view. When she was close enough to see the whites in their eyes, Eva hit the footbrake and the van came to a sliding stop, three inches from the large gentlemen in question. The men, who had not expected this at all, screamed like little girls and tried to climb the brick wall behind them.

"Don't… do… that… again," stammered Agnus as she grasped around for the door handle. The four ladies exited the van and gathered around the five men who were sitting on the ground, mopping their brows.

"You say you know these guys?" Agnus asked Lilly.

"Yes," Lilly replied. "They're friends of Tommy's from work. He did say that we'd have help to get everything set up."

"Lovely," grinned Eva. "Now come on boys, don't be such babies. I never even grazed you." She grabbed the hand of one man and pulled him up to his feet. Dusting him down, she said, "There, there. That's better. See? No harm done. Now be a good lad and help my friends unload this heavy van. The man, who they later found out was called Toni, was quite aware of how heavy the van was. It was one of the *first* things that went through his head as it came hurtling towards him. At that point, he honestly thought that the van would be the *last* thing to go through his head.

As the men slowly emptied the van and moved all the equipment inside, the ladies took the opportunity to explore their new working environment. The building was about fifty years old and was made of hard orange brick. There was one window on either side of the workspace inside and another six in the roof. The place was a good size, they all agreed, and there was space enough to fit four cars in here, although, seeing the equipment being brought in and spread around, Agnus thought there may just be space enough.

Agnus gazed on the mass of tools and equipment that they had just bought and, once again, became a bit overwhelmed. Everything was moving very fast. Was she really doing the right thing here? Or would this all end in disaster?

"It'll be fine," said the voice of Tarquin, from behind her left shoulder, "and anyway, it's too late to back out now. Everything's in place."

"Actually," Sergey corrected, "this is the last point where you *can* back out. You've still got the receipt for all this junk. Just tell the boys to put it all back into the van and return it. Nobody will think the worse of you for it."

Agnus' thought, "*You two are getting on my last nerve, here. Why don't you just leave me be?*"

"Hey," said Sergey, "you're the one with the imaginary friends, not us."

"*We are not friends,*" Agnus thought hard.

"Oh that's lovely, that is," said Sergey. "And I thought we were starting to have a good repartee."

"Just ignore him," said Tarquin. "This is a good thing you're doing. Yes, it may be difficult; and possibly dangerous; maybe even a little daunting but it's a whole lot better than sitting around the house, feeling sorry for yourself."

"*That's actually a good point,*" thought Agnus. "*Let's do this.*"

Tarquin smiled and slowly disappeared as he danced across the room. Sergey just rolled his eyes, saying, as he faded away, "On your own head be it."

※

Tommy arrived around twenty minutes after the men had finished their task[4]. Lilly, having previous knowledge that they would be there, had taken it upon herself to make up a lunch basket for them. In actual fact, it was an ice chest filled with sandwiches, crisps, teacakes and beer. She even laid on a couple of flasks of tea for any of them who would be driving. It was strange to see the frail girl walking unabashed among these men, feeding them, telling them off when they said something inappropriate and basically acting like their mother. What made her feel even better was that all the men took it. These were five big and very tough gentlemen who were instantly transformed into little boys when in her presence. Agnus suspected that they had felt her wrath before and she smiled.

---

[4] Which Big May thought was very good timing.

Chapter 11: The First Lesson

It was evening the next day and the four girls sat in a small line of chairs, watching Tommy as he began their first lesson. He started off by telling them that this was not going to be an easy job and that they should all prepare themselves for the fact that they may not be successful.

That being said he took them around the five-year-old Ford Escort, which he had managed to procure for them, and told them what all the outside bits were called. Agnus thought that this was a smudge on their intelligence but Tommy had said that he wanted to be sure that everyone had the same information. After he had spoken about wheels, bumpers and side panelling, Tommy opened up the bonnet of the car and hooked it into place.

Telling everyone to gather around, he went into detail about the pieces that made up the engine and their purposes in relation to the whole. He spoke about Head Bolts and Gaskets; Core Plugs and Air hoses; while also taking good care to mention the need for Oil Seals.

That being done, he showed them how to use the big Winch and the small Jacks. Lifting the front end of the Escort up with the big Winch, Tommy took the ladies underneath and explained the workings of a down pipe and three-part exhaust.

"Now," he said when he was finished. "I want to talk to you all about the actual driving of the car. Who's it going to be?"

The ladies all looked at each other, Lilly hoping against hope that it wouldn't be her, or worse, Eva.

"Ok," said Tommy, "we'll start with an easier question. Who's got a driver's licence?"

Agnus, as she looked from one of her friends to the other, noticed that she was the only one who had her hand up. "What about you," she asked Eva.

"Me?" Eva replied, "No, never sat a test in my life."

"You could have told us that before we let you drive the van," Big May groaned.

"It's all fine," Eva said, trying to comfort her three friends, "I've been driving since I was twelve. Started on my father's old Robin Reliant back on the islands."

"Well, that won't help you when applying for the race. The driver is required to have a full Uk licence and there's no way around it.

"I guess I'm the driver, then," said Agnus. "Not sure I'm up to scratch."

"You will be. I've got a mate who works over at the Beeline racetrack. I've arranged for you to have a week's worth of track time, while they're renovating the front buildings."

"Wow," said Agnus, "you didn't have to go to all that trouble just for us."

"It's no trouble," Tommy replied. "I'm just making sure you're as ready as you can be. It'd be a shame to go through all the work of building this girl up to standard, only to discover that you can't turn a corner without turning the car… onto its roof," he qualified.

Everyone thought this was sound thinking and nodded, knowingly. All, that is, except Big May who was thinking about something else. "Did you just call the car a '*she*'?" she asked.

"Yes," answered Tommy, "that's another thing. You have to name her."

"Name her what?" asked Eva.

"Whatever you like," said Tommy.

They all pondered this.

"What do you think?" Eva asked Agnus.

"I don't know," she replied. "It has to be a girl's name, you say?"

"It's practically law," said Tommy, pushing them towards a decision.

"How about Bertha," proffered Big May.

"That's more a name for a truck," replied Lilly, "or maybe a van."

"Serena?" suggested Eva.

"Serenity, maybe?" Lilly suggested.

"I think that one's taken," said Tommy. "By something a little bit bigger than this old Escort."

"I think I've got one that might work," said Agnus.

"What is it?" Tommy asked.

"Misses Ford," she suggested, "you know," she qualified, "like, instead of Mister Ford... *Horse Power?*"

"Yes," said Eva, "we do get it. I'm not quite sure about it, though."

"I think it'll work nicely," rallied Tommy and, in the end, they all agreed that this was what the car would be called.

At the end of the evening, as they all waved goodbye to Misses Ford, the girls were exhausted and felt numb to the brain. They had been given a huge amount of information over the last few hours and they were very glad of their notebooks because of it. Every one of them had detailed notes about the car, now. Every word Tommy spoke was painstakingly taken down in case they needed to be known again. Nobody wanted to make a silly mistake and ruin their chances at success.

In Agnus' notebook, she had done diagrams of the car and parts with wee arrows pointing from one to the other, showing where they belonged. At the back, she had written the name of every part she was shown; with a description of the name's piece. She had always been meticulous which had been very helpful when climbing the working ladder. Agnus felt there was no reason to stop now that she was retired. She was going to treat this like she would any project and she was going to make sure they did it right. Agnus found that she was really starting to get a grip on all this. Now she had more of an understanding of what made cars tick, or rather *growl*, Agnus felt that they could go forward with an easier mind.

It was all going to be very hard work and they were going to end up more tired than they had ever been before but they would be able to do it. Tommy seemed like the kind of man who took everything at its proper speed. *Get things done right on the first try*, kind of a person. Agnus believed that he would be good for them. He was so calm and so kind, she hoped they wouldn't break him.

As they were all leaving to go home, Big May suggested popping into the local, Findlay's, for a quick half 'n' half[5]. They all agreed that it would do them good to chat about what they had learned in a relaxed environment. It would give them time to get their heads straight again before heading back to their individual homes.

�

Agnus, Eva and Big May sat around a corner stall, while Lilly was sent to the bar.

"Boy, am I knackered," said Eva. "I feel like my brain's melting."

"Same here," said Big May. "That was a lot, he just told us."

"Well, we've all made pretty good notes, so I think we'll be ok," said Agnus.

---

[5] 25ml of basic Scotch whisky with a half pint of house lager to wash it down.

"I'm just glad that we're done for the day," confessed Big May.

"And what about you, eh," Eva said to Agnus, "getting a week going around a real track. That'll be exciting."

"I hope I do alright," sighed Agnus. "I can drive well enough but I'm not sure how I'll do on a real track."

"I'm sure you'll do fine," Big May replied. "You'll get the hang of it in no time."

"I do hope so. It'll be a shame, *as Tommy said*, if we get as far as having a working car and end up having nobody to drive it."

"It won't come to that," shot Eva, "you're going to be fantastic and we're going to show all these other teams what this bunch of misfits can do."

Agnus smiled. It was always nice to get a rallying call and this one did the job. "Quite right," she agreed. "We'll not just make it to the starting line, we're going to be awesome."

"You know," said Big May, "in all the time I've known you, you've never used the word *'awesome'* before."

"It felt appropriate," Agnus replied.

When Lilly arrived back at the corner stall, the three ladies were in good fooling, even to the point of helping the young girl with her laden tray. As they looked, they saw that it contained four half lagers, three whiskies and a silver aftershock.

"I didn't know you were into taking shots, Lilly?" said Agnus, surprised.

"That's mine," cooed Big May, as she exerted herself, grabbing the small plastic glass and throwing it back in one go. "Ahhh, that's better," she said, as the liquid hit her stomach. She looked happily at her friends, who were giving surprised looks in return. "It tastes just like Calpol," she said, as some sort of explanation.

"Calpol?" asked Eva. "You mean that cough mixture you give to kids?"

"That's the stuff," confirmed Big May.

"Let's see it," said Agnus, interested.

"Well, it's all gone now," Big May replied.

"Lilly," Agnus asked, "do you think they've got any more of that, back there?"

"I'm sure they have plenty," replied Lilly.

Three hours and a bottle of silver Aftershock later, the four girls were still seated around the same corner stall, only now they were a bit more… let's be polite and say, 'sloshed'. To put it a little less politely, they were three sheets to the wind and they all agreed that Calpol was the best flavour of any drink, ever and gave many a toast to the guy who invented it.

"This is the life," came the happy voice of Sergey. "A nice chilled evening, throwing back some shots."

"Wastrel," Tarquin condemned.

"*Aww, what are you two doing here?*" Agnus thought, through her drowsy mind. "*We were having a lovely time till you showed up.*"

"What?" asked Sergey, "We're not allowed to have a good time?"

"You're the only one here having a good time, now," said Tarquin, cautiously smelling one of the small plastic glasses, wincing when the aroma his nasal cavity.

"*I wish you would just leave me alone.*" Agnus thought.

"Hey," said Sergey. "I've got no problem with all," he waved a hand over the many glasses, theatrically, demonstrating, "*this.*"

"I do," said Tarquin.

"Nobody cares," Sergey replied.

"She shouldn't be getting this intoxicated," continued Tarquin. "It's not going to help her illness any."

"*Do you think so?*" thought Agnus.

"There's nothing wrong with having a few drinks," said Sergey.

"I'm not saying there is," Tarquin replied, "but drinking a quarter bottle of… *whatever this silver stuff is*, can't be good for you. Us just being here is proof of that."

Agnus looked down at the empty bottle. "*Maybe you're right,*" she thought.

"No he's not," said Sergey, quickly, "he's talking rot."

"I am not *talking rot,*" replied Tarquin, upset.

"Yes you are," Sergey continued, "and it's no surprise."

Agnus looked up at the two wobbling entities and then back down to the bottle before scanning the glasses which were spread all across the table. "I think I need to go home, now," she said aloud.

Chapter 12: The Hangover

Agnus awoke the next day, with a terrible headache and a tongue like the sole of Ghandi's flip-flop. She got out of bed, *very carefully*, and went through to the bathroom for a glass of water. Every step hurt and every joint felt a great deal stiffer than usual. Due to the girls' unexpected night out, Agnus remembered that she had forgotten to take her medication. She hoped there would be no adverse effects. Agnus took her pills, there and then, before washing and brushing her teeth; more so than ever before as she tried to remove the fur from them.

She strained to remember what had happened the night before. They had left the lockup and gone down to the pub for a quick one. That was clear enough but the rest of the night… *not so much*. Agnus tried to picture the night in her head. There were all the silver drinks; the empty bottle; and the irritating faces of Sergey and Tarquin. The night was basically a blur but these things stood out and she didn't like it.

Never before had she drunk so much. It helped, she supposed, that it tasted nice. The palate still lingered, even now. Every time she took a sip of water, it was like drinking the silver stuff all over again.

Agnus was glad that she didn't have anything to do that day. It was Saturday and that meant that Charlie and Liam would have their heads in the engine of their entrant into the rally. She would have the place to herself and it was a blessing, what with the state of her head at the moment and her uncontrollable urge to throw up. She didn't want anyone to see her like this.

Agnus, now seated on the couch and watching The Chase, felt like she had embarrassed herself, the night before, and was feeling pretty low.

"It'll pass," said Sergey.

Agnus jumped out of her skin. Sergey had popped up, next to her on the couch. He was so close, in fact, that there was a tentative moment. For, when Agnus turned her head to give a witty retort, she found herself staring into the Daemon's eyes, the tips of their noses barely a centimetre from each other.

"I think we need to have a wee talk about personal space," said Agnus. "*Back off.*"

Sergey slid nonchalantly across the couch, away from Agnus. "Is that better?" he asked.

"I can still hear you," replied Agnus. "If you could just bog off, that'd be great."

"Language," condemned Tarquin, popping up on a chair to Agnus' left.

"Well, really," Agnus replied. "He's not pleasant company, in the least, and I'm getting pretty tired of your face too."

"Well, I never!" Tarquin gasped.

"And you never will," replied Agnus. "Now why are you both here again? I just wanted today to be a time of peace and quiet."

"We don't always get what we want," said Sergey, haughtily as he sulked.

"I think…" said Tarquin, quickly before Agnus could react, "that the drink has had a hostile influence."

"Yeah," agreed Sergey, smiling, "you'll be seeing a lot more of us, before the end."

Agnus groaned and grabbed Sergey by the back of the neck. Sergey squealed disapproval, saying, "Here, you can't do that! I'm just a figment. You shouldn't be able to touch me."

"You're *my* figment," Agnus replied, "so basically I can do whatever I like to you. If I should happen to want to beat you up, there's nothing on God's green earth that will stop me from doing so."

Sergey gulped.

"Now, listen here," continued Agnus, "You are going to go away, right now, and leave me in peace. I'm taking charge. No syndrome's going to take me early."

"Fair enough," said Sergey as he vanished.

She turned towards Tarquin. "And you can sod off too," she said.

"I think this is a good step," replied Tarquin. "Taking control, I mean, not the recurring hallucinations."

"You're not helping," said Agnus.

"Now you're going to help yourself. Healthy living and all that; and always remember to keep off of the funny coloured drinks."

Agnus went to give a witty retort but, before she could, the Angel had vanished with a slight *#pop*.

"Thank goodness for that," she said. "Maybe now I can rest my head."

In her moment's madness, Agnus had come to the realisation that she was going to have to start taking better care of herself. She could feel the effects of the drinking distressing her illness. Her joint stiffness and pains were something that came as part and parcel of Lewy Body and she didn't want to exacerbate it in any way.

Agnus made herself a cup of tea and a scone and set herself up in front of the television, once more. The chaser was one question away from knocking out his fourth contestant in a row. As he sat there, leaning casually on his podium, he looked very confident. If the contestant got the next question correct, however, she would be the first to win the round today.

Bradley held the card up. "What," he asked, "is the warning given to visitors as they leave the 'Table Mountain

National Park' situated in Cape Town, South Africa? Is it A. Thank you. Please come again; B. Removing animals from the park is strictly prohibited; or C. Please look under your vehicle for penguins?"

By the time he had spoken the words, Bradley got that look again. He was trying desperately not to laugh and his face was going red. He must have had some producer in his ear because he was trying his utmost to move it along.

"So, Sally, what... do you think the... answer is?" Bradley squeaked, through suppressed hysterics.

"Well, initially thought it might be B," said Sally smiling at the poor presenter, "but I thought that C was too random not to be real."

"Ok," said Bradley, getting himself together. "So, the correct answer is..."

The music came on and the screen flashed.

"C," Bradley shouted, "*Please look under your vehicle for penguins*. Congratulations, you take five thousand pounds through to the next round."

Agnus sat and watched the rest of her show in peace and felt all the better for it. She was going to live life a little healthier from now on. Eat and drink right, and concentrate on getting this car ready for the race were going to be her utmost thoughts from henceforth.

Chapter 13: The Racetrack

On Monday morning, Agnus woke up fresh and ready to start the new week. She was feeling more herself again, after a couple of days rest and remembering to take her medication. She felt bright and was looking forward to her first day of training, over at the Beeline racetrack. She was a bit anxious but was willing to give it her all.

She washed and dressed and had breakfast. Packing a small bag, she set the timer on the DVR to record her show. She'd need something to wind down to after the exciting day she was going to have. Bradley was always a pleasant distraction.

Charlie gave her a lift down to the bus station where she would continue on alone. He had offered to take her the whole way but she was adamant that it was something that she needed to do herself.

The bus ride was agreeable enough with only a couple of other passengers on board. One was an old man of, what looked like, ninety years of age. He was small and hunched and generally looked dishevelled in his loose fitting suit. His face had an air of silent surrender.

The second passenger was a young boy, a big bunch of flowers in his hand and a ring in his nose, who sat staring out of the window all through the journey, listening to some pop music on his chunky headphones. Judging by the mass of flora and the fact that the pierced boy was wearing a shirt and tie, Agnus guessed that he may be about to propose to someone special. Also, she had seen him pat his pocket, a number of times, checking that whatever he had in there was still safe. He seemed to be taking it seriously and Agnus wished him all the luck in the world.

They all got off of the bus at the same stop, each of them making their way to the racetrack of their own volition. Agnus went through the main gates; the old man took the side entrance; and the young boy just stood outside, sucking nervously on a handful of mints.

Agnus made her way over to a group of people who were standing out of the way, having a sneaky smoke. They were all in overalls except for one girl who could be no more than twenty-five, sporting a very elegant striped pantsuit.

"Excuse me," she asked the group in general, "would you be able to tell me where I can find a Terry Cosgrove?"

"Are you Agnus?" asked the pantsuit.

"Yes," Agnus replied, "I was told to meet Mr. Cosgrove around here somewhere."

"Don't worry," the pantsuit replied, "you are expected. Terry's over at the new stands. I'll take you to him now."

"Thank you," said Agnus, "you're so very kind."

The two of them walked off towards the new stands where a great deal of groundwork and construction was taking place. At the edge of it all, two men in orange hardhats stood, pointing at the construction work. They were holding a big piece of paper between them and discussing the new build.

They didn't see the two ladies arriving and so the pantsuit, who Agnus now knew was called Hannah, tapped one of them on the shoulder to get his attention. "Terry, this is Agnus, the lady that Tommy was speaking about."

Terry looked at Agnus who was clutching her handbag in front of her with both hands, nervously twisting the leather handles. "Ah," he said, smiling, "the lady who wants to learn to drive."

"I know how to drive," said Agnus, indignantly. "I want to learn how to drive around a track and not die."

"That's a good aim," replied Terry, still grinning like a Cheshire cat. "What I always say when getting into the car, is that getting back out of it again in one piece is the prime objective."

"Are you going to be ok?" asked Hannah.

"I think we're going to be just fine," replied Agnus, smiling.

✧

After a quick chat, Terry led Agnus across the grounds and over to the garages on the other side. There, she saw five old beaten-up Escorts. Agnus looked at Terry inquiringly. "Am I driving one of these?" she asked.

"All of them," Terry replied. "They were meant for scrap but Tommy did me a favour a while back so, with a bit of love from my friends here," he indicated the mechanics who were standing around the vehicles, "they're fit enough for you to be practicing in."

"Wow, thanks very much," said Agnus.

"Don't mention it. You and your pals are intriguing and, in any case, these being due for the scrappers anyway, you can do what you like with them. Kill them all, for all it matters."

Terry was still smiling so she guessed he meant it. That could be a good thing. She had seen the accidents on the video and she was well aware of what happens if you don't take a corner in the right fashion. Usually, it would be a visit to the emergency room of the nearest hospital. It would be nice to learn how to take corners without having to worry about keeping the car scratch free.

She walked up to the first in line and looked at it.

"She'll work a treat," said Terry.

"She looks like I feel, these days," said Agnus. "She's perfect."

Terry held up a red crash helmet. "You want to give it a wee go?" he suggested.

Agnus smiled a big smile. "I really do," she replied, grabbing the helmet from Terry's grasp and forcing it over her recently permed head. She then walked over to the first car and opened the front door. The outside was a mess but the inside was quite pristine. The front windscreen, too was without cracks so she had full visibility.

The key was in the engine. Agnus sat down in the driver's seat, adjusted it to fit her wee legs and dropped the steering wheel, in order that she could see over it. Smiling at Terry as he slipped a cushion under her, she turned the key and revved the engine a couple of times. "Sounds great," she shouted through the open window.

"Why don't you take it around the track and we'll see how you do? I'll come with you for the first lap or two until you've got the hang of what you're doing. After that, we'll communicate through the radio. There are headphones and a microphone built into the helmet and I have a walkie-talkie tuned to the same frequency so we'll be able to chat, distraction free. I'll be up on the podium there," he indicated a tower in the middle of the track, "watching you as you go around. I can see every corner from there and I'll be able to get a good idea about where you can improve."

"Sounds like a plan," replied Anus. "I feel like seeing what I can do in this beast. Sit yourself down here, son" she patted the passenger seat, "and let's do this."

"Let us indeed," Terry agreed as he entered the passenger side of the old Escort.

✲

Agnus took off like a bat out of Hell and threw the back end out too much when going around the first corner. She went into a spin and came to a sliding stop on the sandy area, three inches from six piles of tyres.

After Terry had stopped repeatedly slamming his foot off of the imaginary break and his heart had restarted, he turned his head to Agnus and said, breathing deeply, "What… was that?"

"I thought the idea was to go as fast as possible," Agnus said, as way of an explanation.

"This is your first time going around a track," said Terry, trying really hard to stay calm, "so why don't we just drive around, *casual like*, and get used to the car. We'll get into getting you faster a little later on."

"Fair enough," replied Agnus. "I'll go slower."

"Thank you," said Terry, gratefully. "Now," he continued, crossing himself, "let us proceed."

They went around the rest of the track without any other mishaps and, after another couple of times in tandem, along with some simple coaching, Terry eventually let her out by herself. Agnus was finding that she was quite comfortable behind the wheel of this car. Not too big and not too small. It was a great drive. She found that she was able to improve on her lap time each and every time she tried. By the end of the day, she had her time down to something just above reasonable. Terry said that, with a little more time and some serious practice on the track, Agnus would be ready to take on the challenge. He even said that he'd be immensely proud to have one of his students in the race. It was a big event and Agnus had his vote… if votes were in any way taken in this event.

She went home that night skipping. It had been a wonderful day and had given her real hope for being able to complete the task. Yes, things were looking brighter. Now that she'd had a shot in a real race car, she had more of an idea about what the race event would be like. A lot more mud, obviously, but Terry had told her that there was a skid test area at the Beeline where she would be able to practice in wet conditions. Agnus thought this was a good idea. She didn't know what she'd do if she hit a bad patch and slid out. Learning to control it could be a real benefit.

Agnus took the bus back into town and caught another that would take her out to the lockup. The girls were all hard at work with their hair a mess and their orange, oil stained, overalls on. They looked like criminals on a chain gang.

"Hello," she said, as she entered.

The three ladies looked up at her, smiling.

"How did it go?" asked Eva.

"Did you try out a real car?" Big May threw at her before she could answer.

"Did you break it?" Lilly queried, jumping on the bandwagon.

"It went splendidly," grinned Agnus. "I did try out a real car, as you put it and no, I didn't kill any of them."

"There was more than one, then?" asked Lilly.

"Indeed," Agnus replied. "your blessed husband here has made a deal and I've got five to play with. They were all due to be put out to pasture but they've made them work enough for me to get the hang of driving the things and when Misses Ford is ready, he said that I could take it across there and give it a run on the track before we head up for the race."

"Impressive," said Eva, "and you did all this for our Agnus?" she asked Tommy.

"Well," said Tommy blushing, "I just want you girls to have the best chance possible. Not that I'm going soft on you or anything," he added as a qualifier.

"Of course not," said Lilly, standing up and walking over to her husband. She gave him a big hug and a kiss on the nose. "You're my Knight in shining armour, so you are," she said.

Tommy's face turned even redder than it had done previously and he mumbled something inapprehensible in Lilly's ear. She giggled and patted him gently on the chest.

"Right, I think," said Big May, to the room in general, "that it is time to call it a day and head off home before this becomes all romantic and I have to be sick into a bag."

"Aww, mam," said Lilly, "there's nothing wrong with a little romance."

"Hrmph," said Big May as she put away her tools and packed up her handbag.

"No soul," said Lilly, grinning.

The ladies cleaned up from their day, Agnus helping them, and they took the bus back to the centre of town where their respective partners would take over. Lilly's respective partner already being there, she and Tommy drove themselves back to their nest.

"It's sickening, isn't it," said Big May, "all that mushy-mushy stuff."

"I think it's lovely to see a young couple in love," Eva disputed.

"I remember that feeling," recalled Agnus. "There's nothing quite like it."

"It's just lovey-dovey nonsense," argued Big May.

"Not in the least," Eva replied. "You're just sore that it's not you."

"Hrmph," said Big May, again.

The three took the next bus to arrive and spent the journey talking about Agnus' experience at the racing track and the girls' lessons in how an engine works and why their one didn't. They laughed and joked and had a very pleasant time. When they arrived at the station, they were still laughing as they waved each other goodbye.

When Agnus went to bed that night, she felt a sense of having done something worthwhile and she liked it. Things were starting to come into place. What had started as a mere thought had now grown into a whole plan and it even looked like they might just be ready in time. That would be a sight, she thought, the four of them leading their Escort out into the field of play with her, a middle-aged woman in a red racing suit, driving. There would be some laughter, she was sure, but her mind was at a point where the thought that her actually being quite good at this was even a possibility. Her lap times were getting better and the girls seemed to be getting the hang of the mechanical side of things. Tommy was a great help there. He had taken them through the workings of the engine, piece by piece, and explained it all to them in simple terms, making sure they were all understanding what he was telling them.

Yes, it was going well and hope was rising inside her. She even started feeling better just at the thought of it.

Chapter 14: The First Car

Agnus arrived at the racing track bright and early the next day. She was so early, in fact, that Terry had not yet arrived himself. Apparently, he was stuck in traffic and he might be a while, so Agnus made herself comfortable inside the garage where they were working from and waited patiently. While she did, Agnus picked up a biography of Jackie Stewart which lay on one of the benches and started reading.

The book was very enlightening. She had heard of Jackie Stewart before, obviously, but she had never realised that his brother Jimmy Stewart was also a racing driver and participated in the Grand Prix for Ecurie Ecosse. Jackie's life was an exciting one at times but the book also went into the bad times. Everyone has their ups and downs, Agnus thought, but he had a belief that held him through the years and that was why he was great. It was because he kept going and had the confidence in himself to do it. He knew what he wanted and he went out to get it. Yes, a great driver, right enough.

Terry eventually turned up, apologising for his lateness and describing an accident involving three cars which had collided with a lorry carrying a herd of sheep. The load was lost and the sheep had, by all accounts[6], made their way off into this new world in which they had found themselves. It had taken three hours to gather all the sheep together again and find a crane to get the lorry back upright.

Agnus said that it was fine and not to fuss. She had been happy enough reading her book. She told him to take his time getting ready and that he should take a second to grab himself a coffee before they started for the day, or rather afternoon as it would be by then.

---

[6] That being Terry's account.

Terry arrived back again shortly after and they rolled the first car out of the garage and onto the track.

"Today," said Terry, "I want you to concentrate on getting your corners right. If all goes well, we'll get your speed up and go from there."

"Sounds good," said Agnus, as she stepped into the old Escort.

Agnus took off at a reasonable pace and began to make her way around the track, all the while with Terry's voice in her ear, giving instructions. She was really getting the hang of it, going around each corner at a decent arch. Her wheels skidded on a wet patch a couple of times but she managed to get back control and carry on with the lap in question. It was thrilling, going around and around the racing track. The power she felt behind the wheel of the car was exhilarating and she never wanted it to stop.

As the hours went by, Agnus managed to gain in speed and in grace. She was really starting to feel that she had a grip on things. Suddenly, however, she took corner nine slightly too fast and the car went over on its side, then onto the roof, then onto the other side…

The car rolled three times before it came to its inevitable stop. Everyone who watched ran to help. Two men who had been close by, darted up to where Agnus and the car had stopped and ripped open the driver's door, pulling the stricken Agnus out and dragging her away from the smoking vehicle.

Everyone gathered around her as Agnus was looked over. Terry, having exited the tower as if the Devil himself were upon him, arrived and pushed his way through the group of well-wishers.

"Is she alright?" asked Terry.

"She's breathing, sure enough," said one of the men who pulled her out of the car.

"Thank you, Lord," he said, palming his hands in prayer. "Quick, get her inside. Hannah, call an ambulance."

Agnus, who had started to come around, was swiftly ushered inside and seated in the cafeteria with a blanket and cup of tea. Her head was aching and her body hurt everywhere, even her mind felt a little slow. As she listened to people talking around her, it sounded like she was under water. And another thing, *toast*... why could she smell burnt toast?

"That'll be the stroke," said Sergey who had popped up in the seat beside her.

"*Did I not make myself clear, last time?*" Agnus thought.

"I did get a slight impression that you didn't want to see me but I just put that down to the hangover."

"Urgh," Agnus grunted. A young lady rushed over to help her take a sip of tea.

"I can do it myself, you silly girl," snapped Agnus. She realised in time what she had said and grabbed the poor lady's wrist. "I'm sorry, love," she said, "I'm not myself, please ignore me."

The young lady patted Agnus' hand, graciously and went back to her conversation on the other side of the room.

"She was nice," said Tarquin, who was never far behind his Daemon counterpart.

"Away and boil yer heid," thought Agnus, getting annoyed. "I'm sick to the back teeth of the pair of you."

"Hey," said Sergey, "I'm only here because I heard you'd been in an accident. I wanted to wish you well and let you know that, if you stop now, nobody would blame you. Hey, they'd probably even suggest it. It's a dangerous game this and you may not come out of it so well, next time."

"It's true that nobody would blame you if you did decide to quit," said Tarquin, "but think about it. Don't just say, '*hey, I've had an accident and therefore I'll just quit*'. You knew it was dangerous. That's what appealed to you, wasn't it? Also, think about all the work that you and the girls… *and Tommy*, have put into getting you this far. It would be a right shame if you didn't get as far as even starting the race."

Agnus thought on this as she was being checked over by the ambulance men. She had no broken bones which she could have told them and there were no cuts beyond that which could be fixed with a plaster. They did say that she may have had a slight stroke during the accident but they would need an ECG to confirm. They took her away for an overnight stay; to the local hospital where Charlie and Liam joined her as soon as the racing track telephoned them and they found out what had happened.

The doctors confirmed that she had had a slight stroke but said it was nothing to worry about and to take better care of herself. *Maybe racing stock cars wasn't the safest occupation in her state of health*, they had inferred.

In the end, they allowed her to go home with a wheelchair which Agnus was adamant that she did not need and a handbag full of painkillers. Charlie drove the three of them home while Agnus drifted off in the passenger seat. He looked in the rearview mirror and gave his step-son a worried look. Liam returned it but, both of them realising that they were never going to talk Agnus out of doing something that she wanted to do, they kept their thoughts to themselves. It was Agnus' choice if she wanted to continue or not.

As Agnus slept, she dreamed of flying cars. Not ones that were in the middle of having an accident but cars with wings soaring and spinning graciously amongst the clouds. Skies were blue and clouds were white and fluffy. When Charlie glanced her way, as he drove them home on the dark roads, he saw a smile pass across her face.

"Oh well," he said and drove on.

Chapter 15: The Recovery

The next few days were torture for Agnus. She was told to keep to her bed and only to leave in the case of a bladder emergency. Charlie made all her meals and she ate them from a beanbag tray that belonged to Liam. There was an inscription on it which read, "*Relish* today, you can always *ketchup* tomorrow." The first time she had seen it, it had made her smile but every time since, it had become a dreaded reminder that she was laid up in bed.

The crash kept going through her mind too. She kept seeing the world turning again, as she had done that day. She even woke with a start a couple of times each night. Agnus just wished that she could banish the memories from her mind and carry on but it was more difficult than she imagined. She was sure that if she got back out there and had another go at it, she could get over the horror of the crash.

Stuck in this bed, however, she was going to have to wait until her body healed. True, there were no bones broken but she had had a few bumps and a lot of bruises from the seat straps and the underside of the dashboard. She had been beaten all over and needed to heal. In a couple of days, she'd be fine and she'd be able to fight her daemons. Yes, not much more of this and things can get back to normal.

"Everybody knows there is no such thing as normal," came the voice Agnus loathed. "There is no black-and-white definition of normal. Normal is subjective. There is only a messy, inconsistent, silly, hopeful version of how we feel most at home in our lives."

Agnus stared at him, surprised. "That's pretty deep for you," she said out loud.

"It's a Tori Spelling quote," answered Tarquin. "He's just trying to win you over with smart-sounding drivel."

"Drivel?" blurted Sergey. "I'll not have you mock Tori Spelling."

"I wasn't mocking Tori," Tarquin replied. "I was mocking you."

"That does it," said Sergey. "You're for it, you jumped up cherub."

"Can a cherub do this?" asked Tarquin as he punched Sergey right on the nose.

Sergey, shocked that the Angel had actually hit him, was hopping up and down and cupping his nose in his hands. "You're not allowed to do that," he said, through the blood. "It's in the rules, isn't it? Peaceful and tranquil and all that jazz?"

"You're an abomination," said Tarquin calmly, rubbing his fist, "smiting's allowed, *encouraged* even."

"Well, I'll have none of it in my house," Agnus slated. "Both of you, sit down this instant and start acting like adults. I don't know," she continued to herself, "Children, the pair of them."

Sergey and Tarquin both sat down, cross-legged, on the bedroom floor.

"So, have you finally seen sense and decided to stop all this nonsense?" asked Sergey.

"Leave her be," said Tarquin. "Give her a bit of time and she'll get back up on those horses. You see if she doesn't."

"Why would she want to put herself in danger, like that," asked Sergey, "when there's some more fancy coloured drinks back in town?"

"I do like oddly coloured drinks," Agnus reminisced. "I may try something green next time."

"We noticed you enjoying them," Tarquin replied, scoldingly.

"Yes, well," mumbled Agnus, "I suppose I did go a little overboard."

"A little?" Tarquin asked, one eyebrow raised in disbelief.

"Now you're the one pestering her," condemned Sergey.

"You're both as much of a pain as the other," snapped Agnus. "Now go away," she barked.

The Angel and Daemon looked at each other and disappeared with a quiet, #*pop-pop*#.

"Some peace to think," Agnus praised.

Agnus thought about her accident a lot while she was laid up in her bed. She knew that if she did decide to ride again then it may lead to some more of the same. She also knew that the girls had put so much of themselves into this project and they should be able to see the results of their labour. Tommy too was a Godsend. The ways that young man had helped them was unknowable. Some of it, she was sure, was even now beyond their understanding. If Tommy hadn't agreed to help them, they would never have got this far.

Agnus thought and thought and eventually the time came for her to leave the house and venture out into the world again. It felt good to have the wind brush her face and to have a reason to get out of her inside clothes, or her *comfies* as Agnus liked to call them.

The only thing now was that she had to make a decision. Was she really going to carry on with this racing business or was she going to pack it all in and drown her sorrows in something green? It was a hard choice. She didn't want to give up but at the same time, she didn't want to put herself back in hospital… *or worse*. What to do? Agnus stood there, going over everything in her head, trying to figure out the best course of action.

After a couple of minutes of stillness that would bring real envy to a statue street performer, she looked up and down the street, gripped her handbag tightly and made her way directly to the bus stop. There was no way she was going to let a little crash bring down all their hopes and dreams. She was going to get back into that car and she was going to show it that she wasn't scared. It would be fine... *maybe*; she'd see how it went.

Chapter 16: The Stubborn Woman

Agnus arrived at the lockup with a spring in her step. She knew she wouldn't be expected back at the track this very day and so had decided to break herself in by seeing how the girls were getting along. When she entered, Big May had her head inside the engine of Misses Ford; Eva was welding something on the other side of the room; and Lilly was hammering a side panel beck into its proper shape.

"What happened here," Agnus asked, smiling. "You've all gone native."

The three girls immediately stopped what they were doing and rushed Agnus all at once. They had so many questions about what had happened and if she was going to be alright. None of them believed for a second that she would be thinking about getting into a car again. When Agnus told them that that was exactly what she was going to do, the girls went daft, trying to dissuade her from continuing, lest she kill herself.

"If you don't want me racing then why are you still working on the car?" Agnus asked.

The three girls looked at each other, embarrassed. "We just didn't like to leave a job undone, is all," said Eva.

"Yeah," Big May replied. "We were tasked with bringing her back up to health and that's what we will do."

"We're certainly not suggesting you drive it," added Lilly. "You should be taking care of yourself."

"What I need," replied Agnus, "is to take control of my life. I need to do this but I'll understand if any of you choose not to follow me on this one any longer."

"You're a pain in the backside, Agnus Ferguson," said Big May.

"But we love you for it," Eva added.

"Just don't die," iterated Lilly, "or I'll never forgive you." A tear started to drip down her cheek.

"Aw, come here, love," said Agnus, giving the upset girl a big hug. "Nobody's going to die," she purred. "I didn't even cut myself, just a lot of bumps and bangs. There's nothing to worry about."

After she had calmed Lilly and they got back to talking normally to each other, Agnus asked the ladies to show her around and bring her up to speed with what they had been doing.

Big May showed her the engine, which was partly inside the bonnet of the car and partly spread across the floor. Big May had said that there was a problem getting the pistons to turn; along with a list of other issues with the thing but that she was positive that she could figure it out. If all failed, however, they would have to find themselves a whole new engine before the race took place. This seemed very technical to Agnus who hadn't been shown all this. Big May seemed to have taken to it like a fish to water, however. She looked like she belonged.

Eva, on the other hand, was trying to reattach the three parts of the exhaust together and, after a number of unsuccessful attempts, she had decided just to weld the things together and be done with it. Agnus was amazed to watch her similarly aged friend, iron faceguard on to protect from sparks, welding a car exhaust together with a flame hotter than she had ever seen before. She suspected that, under the mask, Eva was having the time of her life.

Lilly was a surprise too. She was panel beating a door back into shape using what looked like a hand-held sledgehammer. It was funny and very impressive to see the young scrawny girl pounding away at the door for all that she was worth. Being in this place and doing these things was alien to them all, less than a week ago, but now they were becoming real mechanics. It was about time she became a real driver and a real driver never quits, no matter what troubles come their way.

Agnus stayed with the girls for the whole day, being shown all they had learned and even helping out with a few things. Tommy arrived at the end of the day to collect Lilly and was amazed and delighted to see Agnus back on her feet again. He asked all the same questions and Agnus patiently gave all the same answers. She knew that Tommy must be feeling bad about sending her up there in the first place. Agnus told him that it wasn't his fault and that she was fine in any case. "No harm, no foul," she said "and no blame to issue out."

That being done, Tommy said he could at least give them all a ride home. They graciously accepted. Big May, being the Mother-in-Law, took the passenger seat as a given. Agnus, Eva and Lilly squeezed themselves into the back. With Agnus and Eva not being the smallest of women, Lilly found herself in the middle, her knees at her shoulders which were themselves hunched forward.

"Thanks for doing this," said Agnus, "you really didn't have to."

"It's no trouble at all," said Tommy. "Can't have you standing out in the cold waiting for a bus. Isn't that right Lilly."

"No trouble at all, no," replied Lilly, desperately trying to breathe.

For the rest of the journey, they talked about the car and what was still needing to be done (which was a lot) and the lap times of previous winners. Tommy had said that they should be happy just to be racing. To aim for a top time in the race was, in his mind, fool-hardy and could be dangerous. A good time is what they should aim for, not a great one. Agnus thought that this was probably true. It was their first ever run and they should treat it as such.

Tommy dropped each of the ladies off in succession, Agnus last, and continued on his way home with Lilly back by his side. As Agnus waved them goodbye, she felt a warmth inside her. They were good friends, as were Eva and Big May, and she had a love for them all. She just hoped that she wouldn't let them down.

Chapter 17: The Next Three Cars

Agnus arrived at the track determined to get back into the driver's seat, so to speak. Terry was there to meet her and she could see on his face that he wasn't sure about letting her go around the track again, so soon after her accident. Agnus explained that it was something that she needed to do and that there was nothing he could say to change her mind. He was obviously still worried but said he'd give her the benefit of the doubt.

Agnus and Terry made their way to the garage, chatting about what she had done wrong the last time as they went along. Agnus took it all in. The last thing she wanted was to be laid up again and she was going to take every measure to make sure that didn't happen. Taking everything Terry said and implementing it as rule-of-fact was a big part of that.

Terry was very persistent about the speed Agnus took around the corners. He explained, once again, about taking her foot off of the accelerator before the turn and only pressing down on it again once the car and wheels were both pointing in the right direction. He also went on to talk about applying pressure as opposed to simply slamming her foot straight down on the pedal. All these things were important in taking corners and her attempts at using the handbrake to drift, like she had seen in Liam's video, was to be curtailed immediately. Terry had no time for it except in advanced drivers. Agnus was certainly not ready to try it and he was adamant that she not try.

Agnus agreed with everything that Terry said and took it all in, the whole jing-bang. She was determined to make this work and prove to herself that she was capable of doing this crazy stunt. The whole project was now at the point of do-or-die. It was all going to work out or she would do herself another injury trying.

When they got to the garage, the boys had already pushed the second Escort out of its space and had it ready for her. As they got close, she could hear what sounded like someone clapping in slow motion. A second clap joined it, then another and another. As more joined, the rhythm grew faster until a whole applause was escalating from the large group of boys and girls around the car as they watched Agnus coming back to the track.

"They're all glad you're ok," said Terry, as an explanation.

"That was all for me?" asked Agnus, getting all emotional.

It was an overwhelming feeling to have so many of these people showing her such respect and love. This was another reason to keep on keeping on. The work and love these people had all put into helping her learn to drive was a wonder and she was grateful for it all. It was time now to repay all their efforts and make a real go of this. No backing out, no excuses and no regrets.

Agnus thanked them all with a tear in her eye. Their delight at seeing her again was inspiring. They had even got her a cake. When they had heard the night before that she was planning to return, the girls had got together and baked it overnight. It was a huge Victoria sponge covered in soft white icing. They had even crafted a small blue Escort out of icing for decorating the top of the cake. It was beautiful and Agnus complimented them, saying that she really wasn't expecting any of it.

After the celebrations had died down and Agnus had gone around each of them in turn, giving them a kiss on the cheek, Terry and Agnus walked over to the second Escort to come out the garage. Terry gave her a couple more words of advice and Agnus got inside. It felt slightly different from the last one, she didn't know why. Changing the seat position and adjusting the steering wheel, she made herself ready as Terry made *his* way over to and up the tower.

Agnus got her mind set and wrapped her fingers around the steering wheel. When Terry gave the signal, she shifted effortlessly into first, applied the right amount of pressure to the accelerator and, as she lifted her other foot off of the clutch, she took off with a roar. Agnus heard a loud cheer erupt before fading away quickly behind her as she flew forward.

Keeping Terry's words in mind, she took it easier around the track on her first time back. It was difficult at first because she was a bag of nerves, no matter how well she hid it. As she progressed around the track further, she began to feel more comfortable with being back in a car again and her body started to relax. After that, her movements around the tarmac were more fluid in nature and she felt the thrill she had felt when she had first started getting the hang of driving on a track.

Not wanting to have another ding, Agnus listened to Terry's words and kept the car at a reasonable speed, slowing down for the corners when required. When she arrived back at the start, there was one last big cheer before everyone was sent off to do the work they were getting paid for. There was some bitter mumbling from the retreating group but Agnus heard a number of shout-outs, wishing her all the best.

However, the day was bright but for a short time. A little after lunch, Agnus put the second Escort into a spin and, finding herself in the wrong gear entirely, she ended up reversing, at high speed, into the side of an outside portaloo. Agnus was fine and even managed to pull herself out of the vehicle but, after a closer inspection of the vehicle, the boys called time on the old wreck. Apparently, an axle wasn't something they could fix cheaply or quickly.

Terry, with cause for concern, asked her to be more careful and they moved on to the third car. Everything was going well and Agnus was even getting good at the cornering aspect of the race until a tyre blew and the car was flipped onto its side. It continued to slide down the track, Agnus holding on for dear life, until it hit the siding, tipping up on its nose slightly with the force of the hit and slamming back down again. The whole front end was misshapen and, in some instances, misplaced.

Agnus, who was shocked but in no way hurt, undid her straps and shouldered the door open. As she did, she got a wonderful view of the sky. She climbed out and jumped down onto the tarmac. Terry was running across at her.

"This one wasn't my fault," she shouted adamantly at his approaching face, getting her side of the story in early. "The tyre blew and I lost it."

"I know, I know," gasped Terry as he made it to the scene of the crash. "I saw the whole thing. Are you alright?"

Agnus said that yes, she was fine, and not to make a fuss. She did mention, however, that she might need another car. Terry groaned and told one of the boys to wheel out the penultimate car they had for her. "Please don't break this one," said Terry, through the radio, as Agnus took off once again. "At least not today."

Agnus spent the rest of the afternoon working the track and learning to control the car a great deal better than she had done previously. The problem came when, half an hour before they were due to stop, a fox ran across the track, right in front of her. Agnus swerved to miss it and put the car straight off of the track and headfirst into a wall. Steam started coming out the front of the car and Agnus felt like the engine was sitting on her lap.

The boys rushed over and pulled her out, checking her all over before looking at the car. This too was claimed to have been shipped off to the great racetrack in the sky. Agnus correctly presumed that they meant she had killed it. Things were not going well. She only had one car left, apart from Misses Ford, but she was getting better… she was *going* to be better still.

Terry had gone daft and told her, in no uncertain terms, that if she saw an animal on the track again she was to keep going and hit the thing if she had to. It was more dangerous, as she had just found out, to make a sudden and unexpected change of direction at the speeds Agnus was going at. Agnus said she was sorry and, Terry a little worse for ware, they decided to call it a day.

"Don't worry yourself," Terry had said shakily as she left for the day. "Everyone has days like this… well, not quite this bad but you know what I mean. I'll see you again tomorrow and we'll go again. You'll be fine, I'm sure." He went away holding his forehead with one hand.

Agnus wasn't sure if she believed Terry. His words were comforting but his face had a look of being dazed and confused. She really hoped she wouldn't break him too.

Agnus got the bus back home again and made herself an Irish tea, making use of the Grouse that she has received from Big May last year, for Christmas. She sat there, in the kitchen, in silence. She thought about all that had happened that day and of all the crashes. She supposed it might be a good thing that she was getting used to the crashing aspect of it all. If she had an accident during the real race, she would be able to act in a sensible manner and not panic. She knew this was no reason to go crashing her car all about the place but she took it as a gain as well as a loss; no problems, only opportunities.

As she sipped her tea and pondered, Agnus suddenly remembered about her television show. She stood up quickly, grabbed a couple of biscuits from the everyday tin and went through to wind down. Bradley was such a beautiful distraction that her troubled day faded into nothing and she was found, sound asleep in front of the television, the following morning when Charlie got up for work.

Chapter 18: The Final Lessons

The final week of Agnus' training went without too many hitches and she managed to get to the end of the week without destroying the fifth and final Escort. Her abilities grew and, by the time her training was complete, Agnus was going around the track like a real racing driver. She even managed to beat a couple of the younger lads' lap times which put them into a bit of a sulk. It didn't last long though and when Agnus left on the final day, she was waved goodbye by the entire staff who had watched her come into the place as a complete amateur and leave as something resembling *'quite good'*.

She had thoroughly enjoyed the final week of her training and had really managed to raise her game and do it safely. The fact that she'd not had an accident all week was something that filled her with hope for the future race. Terry had, as promised, taken her to the skid test area a couple of times and she'd had a blast as she was finally allowed to use the handbrake. She learned to control slides and the basics of how to drift around corners. It was an exciting time for Agnus and she was going to miss the place terribly.

Terry had said that she could come back of an evening, on Tuesdays and Thursdays, to keep her hand in. It would also help with the night part of the course. *Night driving*. That had been news to her when Tommy had told her the previous evening. She had presumed it'd be timed laps they'd be doing but Tommy explained that it was a twenty-four-hour race. She had panicked at first but Tommy said that she wouldn't have to drive the whole time as it was in the rules that there must be three drivers for every team.

"But we only have one person who can drive," said Agnus, near to having a second stroke.

"Not true," replied Tommy, "you've got me."

"You?" asked Eva and Big May, together.

"I don't think so," said Lilly, furious.

"I think I'm going to have to, dear," Tommy pleaded.

Lilly was still steaming. "What are the baby and I going to do if you've gone and got yourself killed in some race?" she said.

There was a notable silence.

"Baby?" asked Tommy quietly, suddenly unable to move.

"Baby?" asked the three ladies.

Lilly stopped and realised what she had just said. "Oh, I'm sorry," she continued, in a softer voice. "I was going to tell you later. I'm... well... I'm pregnant." She gave a hopeful half-smile as she waited on Tommy's response.

Tommy was silent and still as the news worked its way through his brain on its way to a conclusion. When it finally hit him, what she had said, Tommy's face brightened again and a euphoric smile crossed his face. "Are you asking me to be a daddy?" he asked.

Lilly nodded excitedly. Tommy rushed over to her and they locked in a powerful and warm embrace.

"I love you so much," Tommy said.

"Same," replied Lilly.

After a reasonable few seconds, Big May coughed. "Excuse me," she said. "I don't want to be a pain but we still don't know who's going to take the other two driving spots. It's not like we're able to get anyone else trained up in time."

"It's already decided, I'm afraid," said Tommy as he kissed Lilly on the head. "Sorry darling. The three drivers had to be listed on the application forms and so I had to act quickly as they were already late in being entered into the records. We were lucky to be allowed to compete at all."

"So you put yourself down as one of the drivers, then?" Lilly asked.

"I had to think of two people who were able to do a race like this and who'd be available for free. There aren't that many drivers around with the ability and availability."

"So who's the third driver, then?" Agnus inquired.

"Our pizza delivery boy," replied Tommy.

The four ladies all looked at him like he had a hole right through the centre of his head.

"I'm joking," Tommy continued, laughing. Then he spoke more seriously, "He wasn't available, so I asked Terry if he would do the honours."

Agnus' heart lifted. The thought of Terry joining her in the race was wonderful. Having him and Tommy both helping her to do this was just what she needed. When she had believed she would have to do the full twenty-four hours alone, Agnus had gotten chest pains and she had started to lose breath. Now that she knew that she would have Tommy and Terry by her side, she was more confident than ever.

"What are you going to drive, though?" asked Agnus. "We've only got the one car."

"Again, not true," Tommy replied. "We've still got that old Escort from the track. You know the one you didn't destroy? Terry's going to get the boys to bring it up to scratch and he'll drive it."

"And what about you?" asked Eva.

"Oh, I've already got a car I can use," said Tommy smiling.

Lilly's face dropped. "No," she said desperately, "not the Charger."

"I'll be very careful," said Tommy, kissing her on the forehead.

Lilly still wasn't sure so she and Tommy went outside for a conversation while the other three cleaned up the lockup for the night.

That was then. Today, Agnus still had her springy step but a twinge of sadness lingered when she thought about not being at the track full-time. She had had a brilliant time there and she wished that she could do it every day.

Now, though, she had to put her nose to the grindstone and help the other girls get Misses Ford into working order. As far as she could tell, they had made great progress but they were having a few problems with the engine and there was a water leak somewhere which they couldn't find. Other things were still to be completed and more still hadn't even been started yet. There was still a lot of work to be done and they needed all hands on deck.

Chapter 19: The Confrontation

The next day being a Sunday, after church, Agnus took her day of rest. Charlie and Liam were out polishing their entry. They were very close to completing their car and, for the remaining time they had before the race, they would be taking it out to a farm in Milton of Campsie for a few dozen test runs. She had heard them talking about a brake-disc that hadn't arrived yet but apart from that they were almost complete.

Agnus started to worry that she and the girls would not have their car ready in time. It would be a hard one to deal with if they failed to meet the entry requirements and weren't allowed to race. She wondered what that would do to the group who had gone through so much in order to get her into the race.

Agnus found that her heart was beating faster and she was getting cold sweats. She tried to relax and put her worries out of her head.

"***This is God calling***," said a deep and echoing voice. "***You're dooooomed!***"

After a second's stillness and thought, Agnus stood up, walked over to the back of the couch and pulled out Sergey by the ear who had been hiding down there. He held a megaphone in one hand (which he had been crowing through) and a dishtowel in the other for muffling his voice.

"What in the world do you think you are playing at?" Agnus asked the hysterical Sergey.

"Oh," he said through tears of utter delight, "oh, that was perfection itself. The look on your face when you thought God was in *your* sittingroom. It was priceless."

"I did not think God was in my sittingroom," said Agnus. "I was just a little startled, that's all."

"No need to feel embarrassed," continued Sergey. "Most people have a wee coronary moment when they hear the voice of the Lord."

"It wasn't the voice of the Lord, you imbecile," Agnus replied. "It was you speaking through this stupid thing," she grabbed the megaphone from Sergey and threw it across the room.

"Don't waste your time," said Tarquin, who had popped up in *her very own chair*, flicking through a newspaper. He had more interest in the articles than he did in her, never removing his gaze from the thing he was reading when he spoke.

"Excuse me?" asked Agnus, affronted.

"I said," repeated Tarquin, "Don't waste your time. He's never going to learn. He thinks that life is just one big game to see who can last the longest."

"What about you?" asked Agnus. "What do you think life is?"

"Life is one event after another. We should do our best in each situation because once that moment is gone... *it's gone* and we move on to the next circumstance. There are no retakes. There is no going back. Doing our best at any given moment and hoping we got it right is the only thing we can do."

"That's very philosophical," admired Agnus.

"Very good," Tarquin sighed, "but do you get my point?"

"I think so," Agnus replied.

"I don't," said Sergey.

"Nobody cares," Tarquin scoffed.

At that point, Sergey made a bad sign with two of his fingers which Agnus took as an affront to her sensibilities and she lost control. She shook the Daemon in front of her, for all that she was worth, and threw him bodily over the couch and onto the table beyond.

"Why don't you just leave me alone!" Agnus shouted at the top of her voice.

There was silence as the blood and adrenaline pumped through her body.

Then... a short cough.

"*Cough*," said Charlie.

Agnus turned around as fast as lightning. "Charlie," she started in dismay, "how... er, how long have you been standing there?"

Charlie stared at her for a second, Agnus' heart beating faster even than it had ever done before. "I think we should put the kettle on," he said, "and have a little chat about how you're doing."

Agnus silently followed Charlie into the kitchen. When he turned around from switching on the kettle, Agnus hugged him tightly. Charlie held her in a silent embrace. After a period of crying and sniffling, Agnus said, "I'm sorry, love. I knew none of it was real and I didn't want you worrying about me. This is something I have to deal with."

"Not alone you don't," replied Charlie, brushing Agnus' hair from her face.

Agnus looked up at the man she loved with all her heart. A weight lifted and her heart slowed to normality. Charlie and Liam were the best things to ever happen to her. She would miss them when she went.

Chapter 20: The New Doctor

Agnus sat in the waiting room of the hospital's dementia unit, Charlie by her side holding her hand. She was finding this really difficult. Her own Doctor, Dr. Cameron, had said that, even though Agnus was aware that these hallucinations that she was having weren't real, there may be others that she wasn't aware of. She had to be careful to watch out for these situations and try to identify them. Agnus didn't know how she was to go about this but she knew that there was a problem and so she had let Dr. Cameron put her up to the hospital for some medical counselling.

Now, she was sitting in the small room reserved for the unit, depressed and scared. The room was small but there were ten chairs, backs against the wall, placed around the room. In the centre, there was a small table with some magazines and leaflets. Most of them were about what services were available to sufferers of dementia of all forms. Posters cluttered the walls, too. These were more of the same. It was all deeply gloomy and made anyone who read any of it, imagine the worst.

Agnus thought it would be a better idea to have some pleasant scenes painted on the walls and maybe have a couple of books to read that didn't involve their eventual and deteriorating future. Charlie was great, though. He was being strong enough for the two of them. When they spoke on the night she had her wee turn, he had said that he had been expecting something like that. When Agnus had been diagnosed, Charlie had read all he could about the disease and so knew all too well what the symptoms were.

After they had been waiting in the room for over forty-five minutes, a woman came into the room in a nurse's uniform. She called Agnus' name and the worried couple followed her out of the room and along the uniformed corridors to an indistinctive grey door. The nurse knocked on the door and a voice on the other side answered, "Enter."

When they walked past the nurse and into the room, they saw a thin woman in her mid-thirties. Dr. Ashcroft, as they discovered her name to be, offered them both a chair before slowly describing what it was that she did.

Dr. Ashcroft was indeed a fully qualified Doctor but had also trained in counselling and so she found her place here in the medical counselling unit. It was designed to help people get through the tougher times of a long-term illness and to try and identify markers where a psychotic event could occur and avoid it.

They listened to her talk for a while and then Agnus described what she was seeing. The counsellor looked concerned a couple of times when Sergey and Tarquin's names were mentioned. Agnus tried to brush it off but Dr. Ashcroft was adamant that it was important for them to study these events. Agnus had replied that she knew all too well what they were about. One of them was trying to help her make the right decisions and the other was being a pain in the posterior.

Dr. Ashcroft had replied, saying that this was all very interesting. She had never had a case come through which involved religious hallucinations and that she was going to take a personal interest in Agnus' case. Agnus had asked if that meant that she had originally planned to just fob her off on some other Doctor? Dr. Ashcroft hurriedly said that, no, no, that wasn't the case but Agnus had seen the excitement in the young Doctor's eyes and she didn't believe her energetic pleads of innocence.

When they left the hospital, Agnus still wasn't very sure about things. Charlie had comforted her and said that they would take each day as it came. Agnus was so glad to have him in her life. He had been a real rock.

Arriving back home again, after an hour stuck in rain drenched traffic, Agnus went straight upstairs for a bath. After a good pamper and a cuppa, she took herself to bed, the worries of the day pushed to one side. There was no use in letting things get on top of her, she thought. As Charlie had said, she should take each day as it came and deal with whatever hit her at the time. Now it was time to sleep and to rest and clear her head.

Tomorrow Agnus was due to go in and help the girls fix Misses Ford. She was determined to be there. Agnus needed a good distraction, to take her mind off of her worries, and that was where she wanted to be. Agnus had had a wonderful time so far with her wee project and she'd be blown if she were going to take her foot off of the accelerator now.

For now, though, she would rest her weary brain and get some sleep. The lavender in the bath oils had done their job again and Agnus was feeling a little drowsy. As she drifted off, she pictured herself racing around the dirt tracks. It was a good feeling and when she finally dropped off, it was with a smile on her face.

Chapter 21: The Hard Work

It was a bright morning when Agnus left to go down to the lock-up. She had put her concerns aside and set her mind to the task at hand. There was still a great amount of work to be done to the car before it would be race-fit but the girls had been working on it non-stop, trying to complete it in time and even now they weren't sure if they would manage. Agnus had promised to help them in any way she could so, toolkit in hand and a mound of sandwiches in her handbag, she marched on through her troubles and proceeded onwards.

She arrived at the lockup just as the rest of the ladies were opening up. Tommy was there too and even Terry had given his time and joined them in trying to complete their mammoth task. It was heart-warming to see everyone muck in.

Tommy explained to her all the things that they still needed to do. The roll cage had been installed and that was fine; and the body of the car was almost back to shape and attached; and they had even managed to fix their problem with the pipes. The problems came when Agnus asked about the engine. Apparently, it was being testy and nothing they had tried so far was helping. They just couldn't get it to run the correct amount of power. It was troubling. What was also distressing was that they had found a hole in the petrol tank; one of the wheels was buckled; the break discs were shot; and there was a strange spark every time they turned on the windscreen wipers.

All in all, they still had a lot to do. Terry and Big May worked on the engine while Tommy took the task of trying to find the spark before it ignited anything. Lilly got her welding torch out and went to work on the petrol tank. Eva took to the phones and started calling around all the garages and auto shops, trying to locate a new wheel and shoulder. Agnus went around the place, all day, clearing away unrequired tools and running back and forth with the ones they did want. At midday, she brought out the sandwiches and made them all a cup of tea.

During their lunch, they discussed what would happen at the race. As Agnus understood it, she would start the race, as the premier driver in the team. She would run for the first four hours, at which point she would bring the car into the pit and Terry would take off and race the next four hours. At the end of the eighth hour, Terry would bring his Escort into the pit and Tommy would shoot off in his Charger. By all accounts, it was a sterling addition to the team. Tommy had been working on it for the last three years and had put a great deal of time and money into making it something to be reckoned with.

Agnus had inquired as to what would happen should one or more of the cars break down. Tommy replied saying that they would have three of the boys from the track to do roadside repairs but if the worst came to the worst and one of the cars was unable to continue, the next driver would have to continue immediately. If they lost that one too then the final car would have to complete the remaining time all by itself.

"I thought that if we didn't have three cars and three drivers then we couldn't continue?" asked Big May.

"That only applies until the race begins," replied Tommy. "So long as all three cars meet the specs, at the point when the flag goes down then whatever happens after that, the race must continue until you are unable to go anymore. It's an endurance race."

After lunch, everyone got back to their specific jobs and Agnus carried on helping out in any way she could find. She watched the others work as she went about and made a point of learning what she could. It was a pleasant time and Agnus found that she felt better for it. The act of keeping herself busy was beneficial and by the end of the day, Agnus was starting to feel a lot more like herself again.

When they left, Tommy gave them all a ride home. Eva and Big May went back to Agnus' house for a nightcap so the drop-off was made easier.

Inside, Eva and Big May followed Agnus through to the kitchen where she pulled out a bottle of whisky and two glasses. She poured her friends a couple of nips each and sat the bottle on the table for them to fire into. Agnus decided to have a Yakult that appeared in her fridge, all of a sudden. Charlie must have bought them.

"So, how are you really doing?" Eva asked after the chat of the day had passed.

Agnus stared at the table. "It's been difficult," she said, "but having this race coming up is helping. It's good for me to have something to aim for."

"Are you really having delusions?" Big May asked.

"They're hallucinations," replied Agnus, "delusions are different but yes, I've been seeing these two young gentlemen."

"Nice," said Eva, winking.

"Not like that," sighed Agnus. "They were more of a pain in my neck. They wouldn't shut up."

"What were they like?" Big May inquired.

Agnus went on to describe Sergey and Tarquin, telling the girls about all the conversations she'd been having with these two infuriating non-entities. She left nothing out and painted quite a picture for her two friends. When she had finished, she looked at Eva and Big May, who had stunned looks on their faces.

"Wow," said Eva, at last.

"Indeed," Big May concurred.

"It's been quite a wild run," replied Agnus.

"So," asked Eva, "Charlie came in just as you were having a brawl with this Sergey fellow?"

"Yes," said Agnus, "it was quite embarrassing."

"I should say," Big May reiterated.

"The Doc said to avoid stressful situations, alcohol and sugars."

"Sugar?" Eva asked.

"Yes," Agnus replied. "Don't ask me why."

"So no blue Smarties for you, then," Big May said.

"Exactly," said Agnus.

The three ladies talked into the night and it was gone midnight before the two friends left Agnus' house, a little bit tipsy but entirely all the better for it. As they toddled down the road, shoving each other out of the way of obstacles, Agnus smiled. It was nice to have two such good friends.

Chapter 22: The New Diet

In the morning, Agnus came down the stairs to find Charlie in the kitchen cooking up a storm. The table was set and there were three small bowls each with a different citrus fruit inside, sliced and ready to eat. On the hob, Agnus could see a bubbling pot of porridge. The aroma was enticing. On the unit, there were also sausages, bacon, eggs, bread, mushrooms and potato scones. Agnus could see that she was in for a treat.

"What's brought all this on?" she asked as she kissed Charlie on the cheek and sat down at the table.

"From now on, you're going to need a decent breakfast inside you," said Charlie. "Tea and toast aren't going to cut it anymore."

"So you're going to do this every single morning, then?" Agnus asked.

"Yup," replied Charlie, "*every single morning* and the rest of your diet is going to change too. I'm going to make sure you stay healthy for longer."

Agnus stood up and gave Charlie a big hug. "We'll be alright," she said.

The two of them then had a good breakfast and it did Agnus a lot of good. She looked forward to more of this treatment. The constant ups and downs of this illness had started to get on top of her and she had begun to feel a bit on the strange side. Dark side of the moon kind of thing. Now, however, Agnus was more relaxed and she was going to enjoy it as long as she could.

After breakfast, Charlie went off to get himself ready for work. Agnus pottered and when Charlie came back to say that he was leaving, she gave him a big kiss to send him on his way.

Charlie left the house with a smile on his face, a good job done. Agnus cherished him.

She went indoors after Charlie had driven off and got herself washed and dressed. Coming back down the stairs, refreshed and ready for the day, she was greeted by a knock on the door. Opening it, she saw Fred, their local Postman, with a handful of letters and a small parcel.

She thanked him kindly and took them in and through to the kitchen. Sitting down, she went through them quickly. She opened the parcel first. It contained a long, multi-coloured, hand-knitted scarf. The monstrosity was a gift from one of her nieces. She had a few nieces and it was difficult to remember all their names. This one, she read on the card, was from a Silvia. A bright girl, as she remembered, but into all this hippy, tree-hugging business that her parents had found their way into.

Agnus moved on to the letters. There were a few *get well soon* cards which was kind. It was nice to know that people were thinking of her. She must remember to find time to put them up in the sittingroom.

At the bottom of the pile, there was one letter that looked somewhat professional. When Agnus looked closer, she saw that it had a return address which was the same as Charlie's work. She opened it up, in case there was something she needed to tell Charlie about.

Pulling the letter out of the envelope, she opened it up, causing a folded piece of paper to fall to the floor. Agnus bent down and picked it up. It was a P45. Why would Charlie's work be sending him that? Agnus lifted the letter and started reading. Her heart broke. It turned out that Charlie had been let go from his work a week previously and this was them sending out his final documents. Why didn't he tell her?

Agnus thought on this for a second before thinking, "Where's he been going, then?"

She put the letters away, wrapped the hideous scarf around her neck and left the house, grabbing her coat and handbag as she went. Ideas were rushing through her mind. Why didn't Charlie say anything? Where was he going when he had said he was off to work? Where was he now? These and many other questions started to get her unsettled. As she ran for the bus, her headache came back and her two self-appointed life-coaches appeared, on either side of her, in their jogging gear.

"Oh no," said Agnus, running to get away from them, "not on top of everything else."

"I enjoy a good run," said Sergey, "don't you?"

"No!" Agnus replied.

"It can't be good for you either," added Tarquin.

"It's not," was all that Agnus could muster, slowing down as she reached the bus stop. Too late, as it happened. The bus driver pulled away before she could get there.

"Damn," Agnus cursed.

"Now, there's no call for bad language," said Tarquin, abashed.

"Away and stick a sock in it," replied Agnus, not amused in the least.

"That's my girl," grinned Sergey.

"You're no better," Agnus condemned.

"Oooo," Sergey mocked. "I hear your man's off doing something he shouldn't be," he added, sticking the boot in.

"No he's not," said Agnus, though she wasn't too sure if she was being honest.

"Quite right," said Tarquin, "he could be doing any number of reasonable things."

"Like what?" asked Sergey.

"I don't know," Tarquin muttered, "but I'm sure whatever he's doing, it'll be innocent."

"How do you know?" Sergey questioned. "You can't know that."

"I have faith," said Tarquin.

"Faith, humph," Sergey mocked again.

"Faith isn't a dirty word," said Tarquin. "Gullgroper[7] is but *faith* isn't."

"I protest," protested Sergey. "I don't take advantage of people."

"That's *all* you do," Tarquin replied, getting exasperated.

"Will you two just give it a rest," said Agnus as she sat herself down under the bus stance.

"I'm only trying to save you the shock you'll get when you find out that I'm right," said Sergey.

"You're not right," replied Tarquin. "You're never right."

"I do have feelings you know," said Sergey.

"Really?" Tarquin questioned. "Can't say I'm sure about that."

"Look," Agnus yelled, "My husband might be off in some place, doing goodness knows what. The last thing I need is you two bickering in my ear.

Suddenly the two miscreants vanished and she was brought back to reality by the sound of a car horn. Agnus looked up and saw, with delight, that it was Lilly and Tommy. She picked up her bag and trotted over to the car.

"How're you doing?" asked Lilly as Agnus got inside the car.

"Oh here and there," said Agnus, just for something to say. She was in a bad place right now and she wasn't quite ready to share. Truly, she knew Charlie well enough to know

---

[7] To grope a gull is an old Tudor expression meaning, "to take advantage of someone," or "to swindle an unsuspecting victim".

that he would never have an affair but he was going somewhere without telling her and keeping secrets was never a good sign in a relationship. She needed to find out where he was going and what he was doing when he got there. The trouble was that she didn't know how to go about it.

She decided that she would put it to the girls, once they had all gathered at the lockup. Maybe they could think of something she could do. Yes, she thought, relaxing. The girls would help her figure this out.

Chapter 23: The Ten-Year Itch

They reached the lockup in good time and Agnus entered after Tommy and Lilly. Eva and Big May arrived shortly after that and they began the day with a hot cup of tea and a scone. The girls chatted casually for a while, all the time Agnus wondering how she should broach the subject of Charlie and his mysterious goings on. It seemed impossible that he was playing away but there was still a wee niggle in the back of her mind, saying, *what if you're wrong?*

Eventually, a break came in the conversation and, as Tommy nipped out for a fly smoke, Eva commented that Agnus wasn't looking too bright of the morning. Agnus explained that, no, she wasn't feeling very shiny and proceeded to explain her marital predicament to her three friends.

When she had finished, the girls all looked stunned. None of them would have expected Charlie as one to be untruthful.

"It's the ten-year itch," said Big May.

"Shut up, Mam," said Lilly. "It is not."

"What's the ten-year itch?" asked Agnus, worried at Lilly's reaction to her mother's comment.

"After the first ten years of marriage," Big May continued, unabashed, "men tend to get a bit restless and go out looking."

"Go out looking for what?" asked Agnus.

"For something a bit more exciting than their current life," Big May qualified.

"It's utter nonsensical alarmist rot," Lilly slammed. "There's no such thing as the ten-year itch. It's just something made up by people like you who don't like to see others in a happy relationship."

"I'm in a happy relationship," said Big May. "Your father and I have been in this a while now."

"Yeah, and he never played away, did he," Lilly added.

"He knew what would happen to him if he did" replied Big May.

Eva commented that she had always found it odd that Big May should marry such a small and nervous man when she herself was, what was the best way to say it?.. *Healthy?*

"It's not my fault, I'm a plus sized woman," replied Big May, affronted. "I retain water."

"You retain pastries," Lilly rebuked.

"Watch your mouth," Big May replied. "You're not too old to go over my knee."

"I bet you've got a doughnut of some kind in your bag, right now," Lilly surely guessed.

"That's neither here nor there," Big May went on, feeling like she was being picked on.

"Anyway," said Agnus, jumping in, "none of this really helps me."

"If you really want to find out what he's up to," offered Eva, "you should just follow him in the morning and see where he goes."

"That's a good idea," Lilly continued. "Just make sure that he doesn't see you."

"Very important in a stalking situation," Eva agreed. "If the prey gets wind of you, it's all over."

"She's not going out on the moors on a deer hunt," argued Big May, who was still unhappy about the comments about her weight.

"It's a relevant metaphor," Eva replied, indignantly.

"Anyway," Lilly continued, giving Eva and her mother a cross side-look, "we'll all come with you. I'll borrow a car from the garage and meet you across the road from your house when Charlie leaves in the morning."

Agnus wasn't sure about it in the least. The whole idea seemed a bit elaborate and what would she even do if she saw Charlie doing something he shouldn't? In her current state of health, confronting him right there and then may not be the best option. She might have an episode and end up back in the hospital again or, *even worse*, those two irritants may even turn up again and Agnus couldn't be having with that.

They went on with their day, after that, putting their minds to the task at hand. The car still needed a lot of work as they knew all too well. At the end of the day, however, the girls got together again and made their plans more official for the next morning.

"If we're all off following Charlie across the city," asked Agnus, "who's going to be here working on the car?"

"It won't take us long to find where he's been going," replied Eva. "We'll come back here afterwards and just stay back a couple of hours at the end of the day."

Agnus eventually gave in and the plan was made. Lilly, Eva and Big May would collect the car and park up across from Agnus'. They would wait for Charlie to leave and the four girls would follow him to wherever he went.

Once they had got the bus home that night and said all their goodbyes, Agnus went into the house and gave Charlie, who was waiting in for her, a brief conversation before rushing off to her bed to be alone. She couldn't be around him at the moment, what with all the worries that she had going around and around her addled mind.

Agnus fell asleep that night, upset and crying quietly into her pillow. Life, over the last while, had been more than a little difficult to cope with. The variable issues with her illness and the car crashes etcetera were all bad enough but now she could be having troubles with her marriage. This was something that she had held onto since hearing the bad news from Dr. Cameron. It was something that kept her fighting and Charlie had been so kind and caring during her bad times. If she were to lose him then she wasn't sure that she would be able to continue, alone.

Regardless of her fears, Agnus closed her eyes and tried to sleep. Rest was important in her situation and it did her no good to go over things in her head again and again. She wasn't going to get any answers until the morning; then it would be a different story. One way or the other, she would find out the truth about her husband and his secrets.

Chapter 24: The Woman in Red

The next morning was very similar to the previous one. Agnus woke up to the memorable aroma of porridge and grilled bacon. She followed the smell downstairs and found Charlie was in the kitchen again, singing as he made breakfast.

"Somebody's bright this morning," said Agnus, quietly.

Charlie turned around, smiling. "Morning," he greeted. "Did you sleep well?"

"On and off," Agnus replied. "A lot on the mind at the moment."

"I'm sure there is," Charlie replied, ignorant of Agnus' true concerns.

Agnus sat herself down at the kitchen table and watched him carefully as he scurried around the kitchen, preparing. She could see nothing on his face but happiness and contentment. Maybe she was wrong about the whole situation. Maybe there was a very simple explanation for the P45 and she was taking this all out of proportion. Agnus started to think that following Charlie might not be the best course of action and perhaps she should just ask him straight out what was going on.

"Yeah, like he'd tell you if he was getting his milk somewhere else," said the nuisance, Sergey.

Agnus sighed. She was getting all too readily annoyed with the hallucination side of her illness.

"If it's a simple answer, I'm sure he'd be happy to explain," Tarquin suggested.

"Yeah but when is it ever innocent," asked Sergey. "Lies are bred from secrets and most secrets are of things that people shouldn't be doing."

"People?" inquired Tarquin.

"Hey," said Sergey, "I never lie. Don't need to. I'm expected to do the things that humans aren't allowed to do. I've got nothing to lie about. It's not like I sneak out, late at night, to help out at a soup kitchen or anything."

"I see your point," Tarquin accepted, "but I really think that, if you give him the chance, Charlie could put this all to rest, right now."

"Unlikely," Sergey disagreed.

"I'm afraid I have to agree with Sergey on this one," thought Agnus, slowly.

"What?" asked a very surprised Sergey.

"I don't like it," Agnus thought continued, "but I reckon the only way that I'm going to get to the truth and believe it, is to follow him on his way and see for myself where it is that he's taking himself when he isn't at his work."

They finished their breakfast with Sergey and Tarquin carrying on a whispered argument in the corner of the room. Afterwards, Charlie made to get himself ready for his imaginary job, so Agnus took the opportunity to peek out of the still closed curtains, to see if the girls had arrived. They had and they were driving something that Agnus would never have expected.

They were parked a little up the street, underneath a gathering of trees. This, however, only made them more noticeable to the general public because the car they had arrived in was a bright green Skoda Octavia with a red dragon painted on the side. There was also an impressive statuette rising from the tip of the bonnet, like you get on some classic cars, in the shape of a bird.

Agnus sighed. If they managed to follow Charlie in that thing without being noticed, then it would be a miracle in itself. She didn't know what they thought they were thinking, sometimes. All this working with cars must have rubbed off and it was starting to go to their heads.

Hearing Charlie cross the upper hallway, Agnus quickly fixed the curtains and made like she was heading upstairs.

"See you later," she said, as they passed on the stairs. "Have a good day at work."

"Thanks," said Charlie, smiling. "I'll see you when you get back, this evening."

Agnus watched as he left the house, closing the front door behind him. Instantly, she threw off her dressing gown which was covering the fact that she was already dressed, shoved her shoes on and ran out the back door, grabbing her coat along the way.

Agnus ran around the side of the house and only stopped when Charlie's car was in view. He had been stopped momentarily by one of the neighbours who was out washing his path. While they were in conversation and Charlie's back was to her, Agnus took her opportunity and crept through the bushes and out onto the road. Rushing across the street, she dived into the empty front seat that had been reserved for her.

After she had got her breath back, Agnus looked over to Lilly who was sitting at the wheel. "Firstly," she said, "you've got no licence so I'll be the one driving. Secondly, where on earth did you get a hold of this thing?"

Lilly blushed with regret. "I just didn't want Tommy to know we were following his mate across the city in it. He might judge, so I told him we needed the car to practice with. I didn't know he'd give us something like this."

"Well it does stick out a bit," replied Agnus, concerned that they might get caught.

"It'll be fine," said Eva. "Just make sure we stay a good distance back and he'll never notice. People don't actually check their rear view mirrors very often. Tommy told me that."

As they discussed this, Big May noticed that Charlie had concluded his conversation with the talkative neighbour and was now getting into his car. "It's too late for anything else now," she said. "Agnus, get yourself in that driver's seat and let's go."

Agnus and Lilly both jumped out of the car and ran around the back of the vehicle, switching seats. Just in the nick of time, they got back in the car and fired their seatbelts into their sockets. As they did, Charlie started forward and on towards his clandestine destination.

Agnus started up the Skoda and slipped into first gear. "This is it," she said, her eyes squinted and fixed on Charlies moving car.

"Just take it easy and we'll be alright," said Eva. "Now, come on or we'll lose him before we've even started."

Agnus pressed down on the accelerator and lifted her left foot off of the clutch. The Skoda shot forward and they caught up, close behind Charlie, in a matter of seconds.

"Slow down, will you," Big May shouted from the back. "He'll see us if you keep driving like that."

Agnus came to her senses and slowed down to a reasonable speed, three cars behind Charlie.

They tailed him right across the city. Charlie stopped only once to pop into the supermarket and came out holding three bunches of brightly coloured flowers. They spent twenty minutes on the bypass alone and when they had been on the road for almost an hour, Charlie pulled into a long lane, lined with fir trees, which led to a very fancy hotel indeed. The place looked like it would be fit for Her Majesty herself.

As they parked the car in a spot where they could observe what Charlie did, they saw him get out of his car and walk towards the main doors of the building. As he approached, a woman wearing a fancy red dress, about ten years younger than Agnus, came out of the hotel to meet him. Charlie passed her the flowers and she kissed him on the cheek.

"What kind of a woman's worth three bunches of flowers?" asked Big May.

"Shut up," said Lilly. "I'm trying to hear what they're saying."

Unfortunately, the words could not be heard. They did, however, watch as Charlie followed the woman into the hotel as she re-entered holding the flowers up to her nose.

The girls remained watching the doors as they closed behind the two players in this sad story, unmoving and silent. Nobody knew quite what to say.

"What do you want to do now, Agnus," Eva asked softly.

"I... I don't know," said Agnus. "I can't believe it."

Everyone seated themselves properly in their respective positions. Agnus sat in the driver's seat of the shiny green 1.8 litre Skoda Octavia, her hands gripping the steering wheel for all that she was worth. The confusion turned to recognition which, in turn, turned to anger. Red hot anger. She looked briefly into the rear-view mirror as she clicked her own seatbelt in, shifted into reverse and took off in an instant, backwards. When she grabbed the handbrake and did a sudden one-hundred-and-eighty-degree turn without slowing down, Eva and Big May were thrown across the back of the car. By bad fortitude, Eva was the one who was crushed between Big May and the back driver's door. They quickly dragged themselves up and locked themselves back into their seats. These two stout Protestants took the brief opportunity to cross themselves, just in case, before Agnus tore out of the old lane and into moving traffic.

The car sped through the streets and onto the bypass at breakneck speed. The three girls were screaming for Agnus to stop but the blood that was pumping through her brain, at the thought of Charlie with some other woman, wouldn't let her hear them. Agnus heard none of her friends' pleas or screams. All she was aware of was the road.

What she had seen, kept running past her eyes. The flowers, the swanky hotel, the kiss, she couldn't get it out of her head. Agnus stared at the road as she sped along and completely failed to notice the police car that had started following them, its lights turned on and its siren blaring.

Eventually, the police pulled up beside Agnus and the girls. The look on his face was priceless as he saw who was driving this bright green racing car. He had a good idea of what he was expecting to find and it certainly wasn't three grannies and a young mum. He honked his horn a couple of times and motioned for them to pull over. Eva and Big May were in the back seat, still banging on the window for help.

Agnus came out of her daze for a second. A second was all it took. When she saw the irate police officer shouting at her to stop, her brain kicked back into action and she swerved the car away from him and off of the road, into a ditch.

The four ladies sat there, as still as the dead, contemplating their future criminal records.

"Well," said Eva, "this is another fine mess, you've got us into."

Agnus dropped her head in mental exhaustion and cried. She was still crying when they were carried off in the police cars and taken down to the local station for processing. Dangerous Driving, Reckless Endangerment, Driving without proper insurance or tax or MOT, Breaking the Speed Limits and Resisting Arrest, were not good charges to have all in one go.

When they had been fully processed, placed in the cells and the door firmly locked behind them, Agnus lay down on the only bed and, almost instantly, faded off to sleep.

Chapter 25: The Jail

When Agnus awoke at four pm it was to the chilly company of her three friends. At least, she hoped that they were still friends. The events of the morning may have changed their ideas on the fact. By their faces, she could tell they weren't happy and Agnus couldn't blame them. She had gotten so angry at Charlie's unfaithfulness, that she had quite literally seen red as her bloodshot eyes proved. She lost control. All she saw was the road and the images in her head.

She had calmed down now, of course. The sleep had done her good. The girls, however, didn't look like they had had much rest. They were all looking completely miserable and defeated, with their hair a mess and their makeup rubbed off in parts. They cared not.

"I'm sorry," said Agnus, honestly. "I kind of lost it earlier on."

"*Kind of lost it,*" Big May imitated. "Yeah, I'd say you lost it alright. Those bleeding coppers were chasing us for ten minutes before you found yourself back in the real world."

Agnus felt awful. "I really am sorry," she said, apologetically.

"I know it was hard," said Eva, "to see Charlie and that girl but you lost all control of your mind. We were all terrified for our lives, you silly sod." She started to cry.

Agnus gave her a big hug. "Don't cry," she said, "you'll set me off next."

"You're too late to be next," said Lilly, solidly as she crossed the room to comfort her mother who, even with her tough life growing up in the council estates, had never been so close to death than when she was inside that car."

Agnus felt as bad as she possibly could. Her illness and the racing cars; the problems and the crashes; Charlie and this other woman; they all played their part in her sudden breakdowns and it pained her to think that she had put her friends in danger because of it.

Eventually, they all forgave her and they turned their unified distress in the direction of the Cell Officer. They called him over and demanded to be released. His reply was to hit the bars with his nightstick and say that they would only be let out if and when their bail had been met. All four of the ladies' next of kin had been contacted and they weren't going anywhere till their families arrived to get them out.

For another two hours, they sat in the dark and funny smelling cell before the Officer came back and opened the gate. All four ladies got up to leave but Eva was held back.

"What's your problem?" she asked the annoying little copper.

"I'm afraid you're staying," he said. "You've got a warrant out for your arrest," he informed her.

"For what, pray?" Eva asked.

"I can't go into details but it involves three litres of French Whisky and robbing Chief Inspector Williams of the Metropolitan Police, London, of all his clothes but his undergarments."

"Oh, that?" answered Eva, recalling the happy memory. "He knew that was only little old me," she smiled cheekily. "We were skinny-dipping in the old pool out the back of my parents' home, twenty years ago. It was a different time, then," she finished in happy memory.

"I'm afraid I still have to hold you," said the Officer. "A warrant's a warrant, even if you do happen to be telling the truth, which I don't believe for an instance. We'll see what the Chief says when he gets here."

Eva smiled brighter than before. "Willie's coming here?" she blushed. "You don't happen to have a brush and maybe a spot of lipstick do you?" she asked the now weary Officer.

"No," he said, sourly, "now sit yourself down while I get your friends discharged."

The other three girls followed the Officer out of the cells and up some stairs until they reached the ground floor. Going through the doors that awaited them, they found themselves coming into the main reception of the Police Station. Charlie was there with Liam. Agnus decided that she would have her little talk when the boy wasn't around and so played nice, saying that she'd explain everything later.

It was quiet in the car home. Agnus didn't even look in Charlie's direction, choosing instead to watch the lampposts fly by her one after the other, *swish-swish-swish...*

On their return, Liam was sent upstairs to get washed for dinner. Charlie and Agnus went through to the kitchen and sat down on opposite chairs.

"So," asked Charlie, "what happened?"

Agnus decided to let go and the words just burst out of her, "What happened was, I saw you and your fancy lady going into that hotel, this morning. How could you?" she cried.

"You were at the hotel?" Charlie asked, nervously.

"Yes," Agnus yelled, "and I saw the two of you getting all misty together."

"There was no mistiness involved," argued Charlie.

"Yeah? Then why were you there, then? And why did your work send you this in the mail?" she slammed the P45 down on the table.

Charlie looked at it and sighed. "I didn't want you to find out till you were feeling better," he started.

"Find out what?" Agnus demanded.

"I've been let go," he said, miserably. "They've given me a few weeks work, at the hotel, fixing up their cellars with new oak panelling. I was going to tell you but I didn't want the news to affect your progress. I know stress is a trigger."

"So what was with the flowers, then?" Agnus asked, still not convinced.

"Flowers?" said Charlie, "oh, Lizzy, the girl you saw, is the front of house Manager. She had given me a call on the mobile after I left, to say that she needed some for display as the Directors of the hotel were due for a visit. I picked them up at the supermarket before I got there."

"Well, you've just got an explanation for everything, don't you," said Agnus, still unhappy.

"It's all true," Charlie pleaded. "I could never run off on you with another woman. You're my life and damn it if I don't love you to bits."

"I love you too," replied Agnus, letting her grief go. She felt so silly. If she had listened to that annoyance, Tarquin, and had this talk with Charlie beforehand, she could have avoided all this mess. Then again, would she have believed him at that point? Agnus wasn't sure.

They stayed there for a while, in each other's arms, both crying. Liam came down a little later when he knew that everything had died down and they ended with the three of them in a group hug.

Chapter 26: The Backstory

When the girls got together, the next morning, it was to a barrage of questions and they were all aimed at Eva. They had all been wondering, through a sleepless night, what on earth the business was with the skinny-dipping police Inspector.

Eva tried laughing off the whole situation and getting on with the day but the other three girls were adamant that they would be able to do no work until the news was known. It was not usual for Eva to keep something to herself so the girls knew it must be something good... *or maybe a little bit bad.*

Eva eventually backed down and they all sat around a workbench awaiting the telling tale.

It had all begun on a warm summer's day, back in the year nineteen eighty-four, when Eva had been a lot younger. Her father was a farmer on a local estate and tended the lands for the owner. Now, William was only a constable at that point, not long up from London, and, after visiting the farm on some minor business, he and Eva started walking out.

It had been a thrilling time for Eva. She had been in her late thirties but she had felt like a young girl when she was with her William. They used to run amongst the fields and grounds of the estate, kissing under a grouping of trees which would always be their own special place.

The troubled day had come when William told her that he was getting transferred back to the mainland and was to be placed in London, once more. Eva had taken this as evidence that he didn't really love her so, after convincing him to go for one last dip with her, she got him down to his drawers and teased him into the water. No sooner than he was in the water than she was out of it. She grabbed all the clothes that sat on the grass and took off, running. She only stopped when she was a half mile from the river, in order to dress and hide William's garments.

Apparently, his Sergeant had taken the issue very seriously, as William had been in his uniform at the time, and called out a warrant for her arrest. Not being known to the rest of the constabulary and the locals being no help at all, Eva had managed through life without having to deal with it. When she was arrested the day before, however, a buzzer had gone off somewhere and she was held back until one of the named Officers named on the rap sheet could come down and deal with her.

Fortunately for Eva, the old Sergeant had long since retired and William was the next one on the list to call. He had come down to the station very quickly and was wearing the biggest grin when he saw Eva looking at him through the iron bars.

Eva talked him around with her usual wit and saucy flare and two hours later they were having dinner at a local Chinese restaurant. They laughed, they reminisced and they had a great meal in great company.

"So, are you going to see him again," asked Big May.

"I'm a happily married woman, now," Eva replied, affronted.

"Nothing wrong with meeting an old friend for dinner, every now and then," Big May argued.

"Just don't keep it a secret from your husband," said Agnus, sadly.

"That's right," said Lilly remembering why they had all been in the cells in the first place, "what happened with you and Charlie?"

"Quite a lot," Agnus replied, "but it looks like I overreacted."

Agnus went on to tell them what Charlie had told her. She explained that he had lost his job, due to cuts, and that he was working up at the hotel for a few weeks to make ends meet. She explained that the girl they saw was a manager there who had asked him to pick up the flowers which the girls had seen him buy. Agnus explained it all and left no detail untold.

When she had finished, the other girls looked at her, sorry for their mistrust of a man who was only trying to look after his family in any way he could.

"I guess we got the wrong end of the stick," said Big May.

"It was all for nothing," added Lilly. "We spent the day in jail and it was all for nothing."

"That wasn't jail, Lilly dear," said Big May. "We were in *the cells*. They're fine enough. Jail is a whole different beast."

"You speak like you know," Lilly queried.

"I wasn't always your mother," was all the reply she got.

"So," asked Eva, moving the conversation on, "are you and Charlie alright, then?"

"Yes, thank goodness. We had a good cry and a cuddle after the fact and we're better now."

"I'm glad to hear it," said Big May. "I've always said he was a good man. One to be trusted."

"You were the one going on about the ten-year itch," said Lilly.

"It's a known fact..." Big May argued but Agnus tuned out. It would take some time before she could call her home-life normal again but she and Charlie were indeed good and all of Agnus' doubts had been squashed. She didn't like that she distrusted Charlie. She knew full well that he was indeed a good man and that he loved her very much. It hurt her to think bad of him and even worse that she was wrong. It would take a lot for her to make it up to him but she was more than willing to try *and she would*.

They started work on the car after a few minutes for Lilly and Big May's "Discussion" and worked the whole day, glad to be back on the job. They found out, at lunch break, that Lilly had had an argument with Tommy on the way home from the Station, Tommy feeling that a trust had been broken when Lilly had lied about needing the car to practice with.

Big May also had a blowout with her man which would eventually pass. He was just annoyed about missing the football to come down and pick her up. She still felt down, though.

Today was a day when everyone was glad to have something to do and something to put their mind to. They worked in silence for the rest of the day and took the bus back home to avoid any uncomfortableness in the company of Tommy. Again, the bus journey was a quiet one and the ladies alighted at their respective stops with a simple, "See you tomorrow," as they departed.

Agnus went to bed that night, tired and a little down, too. It had been a crazy few days and she needed to rest her brain and body both. With the help of some hot chocolate, Agnus drifted off to sleep. Dreams came to her as she slept but they were fluffy and cloudy in parts, making it difficult to see any details clearly. The mind can play tricks on us even when in the land of nod.

Chapter 27: The Irish

The girls all arrived at the lockup, the next morning, a little low in spirit but in good fooling all the same. The determination to continue and complete their huge task was a strong one and they worked with renewed vigour and resolve.

At lunch break, the girls sat outside because it was an agreeably temperate day. There was a slight breeze but it wasn't strong and had a pleasant warmth to it. None of them were interested in talking about the events of the past few days and so conversation stood with tradition as they discussed the day, the weather and the job at hand.

Big May had said that the engine was still giving her trouble. Tommy had had a play about with it too but neither of them could find or, obviously, fix the problem. Agnus had asked what it would cost to get a new engine, if the worst came to the worst, and was put into a state of shock when Big May replied that it would be another five hundred pounds, if they were even able to get hold of even a two litre one, which was the least they would need if they were to have enough power to compete.

That aside, Misses Ford was coming along well. Obviously, there was still a lot to be done before she was match fit but things were taking shape and, engine excluded, they were on track for finishing on time. They even had a shipment of tyres on their way, the order of which had been put through the garage's books for a better price and quality.

Yes, they were getting there and they could see the finish in their sights; well, the starting line anyway. The girls grew more excited as they talked and rested after their morning's work. The spell was only broken when an old Mercedes van was noticed driving down their private path. The girls all stood up as the van pulled up beside them, three men climbing out.

One was a tall strong man in his fifties. The other two were younger. One of these younger gentlemen was a slender man and the other was of the more porky persuasion. Porky had a slight dimness to his gaze as if he wasn't quite there. Agnus thought he looked a few valves short of a wireless.

"Top o' the morning to you, ladies," said the one who was clearly in charge. "Isn't it a truly beautiful day?"

"Can we help you?" Agnus asked, not liking this man from the off. You know how, every so often, you just get this feeling about someone? That's your sixth sense warning you to be careful. Agnus had that feeling now and she didn't like it.

"We are but humble men," said the man in charge. "We also happen to race cars ourselves and when we heard about your incredible efforts," he turned his head and smiled at his friends before continuing, "we just had to come down and see for ourselves."

"Where did you hear?" asked Eva, who also had a bad feeling about these three men.

"Oh, ladies," the man grinned, "you are the talk of the town. Everyone's gossiping about the new, *cough*, contenders."

"I don't talk to anyone who hasn't even introduced themselves," said Big May, stoutly.

"Oh, I am sorry, ladies," the man smiled. "My name is Connor," he bowed, slightly, "and these are my boys Ruben and Derik," he continued, introducing the two brute looking lads behind him.

"So what is it you want here?" Agnus asked, sourly.

"I was just wondering if a lowly car owner such as myself could be graced with a mere glance at the car in question."

"Big words for a thug," Big May whispered.

Connor's face froze for a second before he continued, a little less personably, "Ladies, there is no need for hostilities. I just wish to have but a peak. Surely there's no harm in that?"

"I'm afraid it's out of the question," said Agnus. "The car will be displayed with the rest of them on the night before the race."

"The car's just beyond that door," Connor grinned. "Are you really going to make us wait three weeks to see what it looks like?"

"By George, I think he's got it," replied Big May, fearless in the face of a greater force. These three men would have no trouble pushing them aside and making their own way in. It was only the cheery conversation that was stopping them, thus far. Agnus worried that Big May's comments would cause a crack in the agreeability of this man and trouble could follow.

"I feel I have been unclear," Connor said. "I was not proposing that you have a choice in the matter."

"If you want to see what we've got, you'll have to go through me," said Big May, picking up a foot-long spanner which she had sitting beside her during lunch.

"*Here we go*," thought Agnus.

"Please don't make this any more difficult for yourself, ladies," said Connor. "We will see that car."

"Not on your life," replied Eva, gaining some false confidence from Big May's empowering actions.

Just as Connor stepped forward, with an aim to push his way through, there was the honk of a horn and as they all looked up to see where it was coming from, they saw three cars coming down the path at great speed. They tore towards the group and each one skidded effortlessly into a parking spot. Tommy jumped out of the first car and strode straight at Connor, shoving his face right up to the older man. Terry had jumped out his car by now and had placed himself between the two sons and the four ladies.

"That's my wife and her pals you're messing with Connor," Tommy shouted. "I think it's time you get yersel' out o' here, what d'you think?" He was in a rage and Lilly thought that her Tommy might just pop this guy, right there in the mud.

"Who's going to make me?" asked Connor, pushing against Tommy's forehead with his own, sending Tommy back a foot. Tommy was just about to rush Connor and rip his head off but there was the sound of a stern cough and another one of a car door closing.

Everyone looked at the third car that had come down the way. Standing beside it was a tall, well-built man in a pair of dark denim trousers, a purple open-necked shirt and a leather jacket. He stood beside his car and took a second to pull a cigarette from out of a silver case, slip it into his mouth and light it with the flared spark of a match. Throwing the match away, the man looked over to the group and started to walk casually towards Tommy and Connor.

When the man reached the two squabblers, he put the hand that held the cigarette on Connor's shoulder, holding the other out to shake his hand. "Connor O'Connell isn't it?" asked the man, pleasantly.

Connor nodded. Agnus could see that his whole manner had changed. No longer was Connor the highest in the food chain. Whoever this man was, he was certainly someone to be reckoned with.

"I think you know who I am," said the mysterious man.

Again, Connor nodded.

"Good, good," the man replied. "That makes things go a lot quicker. I think you need to apologise to these ladies and then be on your way. We don't want any unpleasantness, now do we?"

"No, Sir," Connor replied, nervously.

"Go on, then," encouraged the man.

Connor turned his gaze to the four girls. "I'm sorry," he said.

"Right, now on your way," the man finished.

Connor carefully and quickly motioned his two sons into the van and reversed his way back up the path as fast as he could.

The man turned towards the girls. "I'm sorry about that," he said. "Some people just have no respect."

"Er, thank you?" said Agnus, not quite sure what had just happened.

"This is John," said Tommy, explaining. "The two of us went to school together. His father's also… well known in this area. As it happens, it's also his father that's organizing the rally. John's the reason we were able to register after the deadline."

"I was intrigued by your entry," said John. "Tommy painted quite a picture."

"I was actually bringing him down here to see the car," Tommy continued, "when we spotted Connor and his two boys making trouble."

"Well," said Agnus, "thank you, again and if you want to see the car, it's just in there. I'm afraid it's not looking like much yet but she'll be good once she's done."

"I'm sure she will," replied John. "May I?"

Agnus walked John over to the big doors, opened one and let him in to have a gander. To say that he was impressed was an understatement. John found it baffling that a group of woman, such as themselves, could decide one day that they were going to build a car and actually go through with it. John commented on the amount of learning the girls would have had to do in order to get themselves up to this point and congratulated them emphatically.

    John wandered around the lockup, looking at the work the girls were doing. Every so often he would tinker and make a small comment on how to make it better. It was all very nice and so was John. The girls took to him quickly. His charm and personable character were like catnip to them. In the back of their heads, they were all *oohing* and *ahing* and hanging on his every word.

    Big May told him about the problems they were having with the engine. Apologising that his skills were not as good when it came to engines, John said that he would send someone over to have a wee look at it and see what could be done.

    The girls all thanked him lovingly. Even Big may curtsied when he shook her hand. She didn't know why, either. Her knees just kind of gave way and she was doing it before she realised.

    As he drove off again the girls all waved him goodbye, a little sad that he had to leave them. John was nice to have around and easy to talk to. The fact that he wanted to help them in their project and that he was even going to the trouble of sending one of his employees down to check out the engine, fuelled their hearts with hope and delight.

Chapter 28: The Diagnostician

The next day, the girls were back at the lockup, undeterred and itching to go. The confrontation from the previous day had done the opposite of what Connor and his boys had hoped for. These girls, who did not back down in the face of his austerity, were angry at the Irishman's presumption that he could push them about. They were going to finish this car even if it killed them and show this *Connor O'Connell* what the hype was all about, right there on the track.

Lilly received a call from Tommy while they were having their mid-morning cuppa. He said to expect that friend of John's to come around to look at the engine. Tommy also said that there was no need to worry but the guy that John was sending was... well, slightly odd. He wasn't dangerous or anything, Tommy had said quickly, but he did like to be called *The Diagnostician*. Nobody knew why or even cared that much. The girls had said that they would give him a chance but they weren't promising anything.

Getting back to work, they grafted hard and with great force of mind. They only looked up from their work when they heard someone chapping on a steel drum with a stick.

To be more precise, it was a swaggering cane with a dragon's head as a handle. When the girls turned their heads to look at the doors, they saw before them a man who looked like he belonged in a performance of Stomp, if it were performed by Cirque du Soleil. He wore a baggy pair of black denim trousers, to which he had attached both a belt and braces. The braces, however, seemed to be unrequired by the young man because, although attached in the proper way to the trousers, were not hooked on to his shoulders and as such were left hanging in the wind, flapping against his legs when he walked.

His shirt was also black with silver studs but the sleeves had been cut off at the shoulder. Underneath the shirt, which was completely confusing for the girls, he wore a tight fishnet undershirt which stretched down his arm and half way up his hand. There was also a small hole, at the end of each sleeve, for him to insert a thumb. For what purpose, the girls couldn't fathom. Under the shirt, barely visible through the netting, the young man had both arms and shoulders tattooed, all the way down to the wrist. Agnus wondered why a person would want to do this but then thought, *what a world it would be, if God had made us all the same.*

On the top of his head, the young man sported a top-hat which would have looked very distinguished if worn by any other man. On him, however, he looked like a low-rent illusionist. To finish off the whole outfit, this *Diagnostician* had a piercing right below his bottom lip and three more on his nose. His ears, as far as Agnus could see, was clean of them.

In the young man's hand, he held a black leather briefcase, with gothic style straps. The girls all guessed correctly that this was where he kept all his personal tools and the like. There hadn't been anyone yet who had seen inside the case who could name but four of the instruments he carried. To put things a little more acutely, he wouldn't have looked out of place at a steampunk[8] convention[9].

The young man stood there, at ease, holding the case at his side. "May I present myself, ladies," he said. "I am," he paused, "*The Diagnostician.*"

"Are you, now?" said Eva, sarcastically.

"I am," the Diagnostician replied, simply.

---

[8] Steampunk: A genre of science fiction that typically features steam-powered machinery rather than advanced technology.
[9] A large event where fans of the steampunk genre come together, often dressed as their favourite characters from the books, graphic novels, television shows or movies.

"Fair enough," said Agnus, unsure. "Tommy says you're alright and if you work for John, I suppose we can trust you. All I want to know is if you can fix this engine or not?"

"We shall see," replied the Diagnostician. "Please, let me see the patient."

Agnus and Big May shared a look before Agnus nodded. Big May directed the Diagnostician over to the car and explained to him the problems they were having with it. Seeing as the Diagnostician had said that he would need time to solve the problem, the girls decided to take a long lunch. They made a call to the local restaurant and ordered out. Before long they had a beautiful meal brought to them which they lovingly enjoyed, outside in the sun clad carpark of the lockup.

Lilly had the lemon sole which Big May wouldn't stop complaining about. Big May herself had gone for the chicken because, as she said, you can never go wrong with the chicken. Eva who had had enough chicken while growing up to last her a lifetime had chosen a duck compote which Agnus thought looked delicious. Agnus, the last to order, had decided to try something new and selected the Highland Venison with red cabbage and butternut squash. It was a wonderful meal and the girls made a point of calling up the restaurant to make a personal commendation and to congratulate the Chef.

After they had been napping off the effects of their lunch for about forty-five minutes, the Diagnostician popped his head around the door and asked if they were free for a wee chat. He did not look as happy as when he had first arrived and Agnus took that as a bad sign.

They followed him back into the lockup and over to Misses Ford.

"So," asked Agnus, "what's the story? Can you fix her?"

The Diagnostician, realising that this was no time for antics, said, "To put it simply... no. There's a hole right on the inside here," he poked a biro down into the engine to show the girls. It was indeed deep down, making any welding impossible. "It's done, I'm afraid," he finished.

The girls' hearts dropped. So, they would have to buy a whole new engine after all. Agnus had the money, it was true. There was plenty in her account to pay for it but she had hoped to have that money left to pay for any initial expenses her illness brought.

"I can fix it," said a low but lilting Irish accent.

Everyone turned around to see Derik, Connor's youngest, standing half out the door. He had a very *'Fester Adams'* look about him and his bald head didn't help. The podgy man looked nervous as he stood there waiting for their response to his presence. A slow fat boy, thought Agnus. He probably had people bossing him around his whole life. She wasn't sure why he was there, however, standing in their lockup after what and happened the previous day. She asked him as much.

"Father weren't happy," Derik said.

"I'm sure that's true," said Agnus, "but it doesn't really answer my question."

"Father weren't happy," he repeated. "When he unhappy he hit Derik. Derik don't like being hit so Derik leave."

"But why come here?" asked Agnus, feeling sorry for the poor boy but still confused.

"No place else to go," Derik said, simply. "Like cars."

Agnus felt sorry for the poor man. He had a sad look about him and he was obviously nothing like his father, Connor. "Ok, then," she said, "what do you think you can do for our engine?"

Derik pattered over to the car, surprisingly light on his feet for such a stout man. He looked inside the engine and, seeing the problem, he opened the Diagnostician's case and rummaged about. Pulling out a number of items that Agnus couldn't name, he messed about inside the engine for a bit. Bringing his head out again, he removed a long thin and what looked like a homemade attachment from his inside pocket. He picked up the welding torch and attached the attachment to the nose.

He pulled the trigger a couple of times and the girls noticed that the new attachment permitted the flame to be lessened and allowed Derik to weld further down inside the engine, the attachment being so long and thin. Agnus was truly impressed. The skill Derik must have in order to design and build his own welding attachments must be great indeed.

Agnus asked Derik how he had become so good with engines. Did he train? Did he learn on the job, with his father? Derik had replied, saying, "Father don't let Derik drive but Derik like engines."

That was about all they were going to get.

Derik finished up and put all the sockets and tubes back into the correct positions. He then dusted off the top of the engine and dropped the bonnet down.

"Is that it done?" Agnus asked.

"Yes, mam," said Derik. "Six hours, then try to start."

The Diagnostician was so overawed by Derik's skills that he offered him a job, right there and then. He said that he'd even throw in accommodation. Derik seemed all too happy to go with the anomalous man and he followed the dark-clothed oddball out to his car.

The girls, alone now, all looked at each other and sighed in unison. It had been a very strange day in the company of very strange people. It had been, however, a very successful day. Although the Diagnostician had been next to no use at all, with Derik's expert help, they were able to plug the leak and get the engine running, *hopefully*. They would still have to tune it and then fine tune it but that was no real problem, it would just take a wee while to do.

All in all, it was a good day and the girls went from the lockup, happy in their work and hopeful for the future. Things were starting to look up.

Chapter 29: The Teasing

That evening, when Agnus arrived home, she was greeted by an exasperated Charlie and a very quiet Liam. She hung her coat on the peg, popped her hat on top of it and sat down in her chair. She looked at her two boys. "Ok," she said, "what's been happening?"

"He's been suspended from school for fighting," said Charlie.

"What?" Agnus gasped. "Why were you fighting?"

"Apparently, some of the boys, one in particular, have been giving Liam a bit of stick about you and your wee project."

"Oh dear," said Agnus.

"They said you were going to die out there," said Liam, a small tear sliding down his face.

"They shouldn't be doing that," said Agnus, softly, astounded at what kids said to each other, these days. "Who was it? Give me a name and I'll sort this right out."

"I already sorted it out," said Liam.

"Indeed," confirmed Charlie. "That's why you've been suspended."

"They can't suspend a boy for looking out for his mother's honour," Agnus argued. "I'm going down there, first thing in the morning, and I'm going to have a word with this Headmaster of yours. You'll be back in school before the day's out."

"You couldn't leave it a couple of days," suggested Liam.

"Why, son?" asked Agnus.

"There's a trig test on Wednesday and I'd prefer not to be there when it happens."

"You'll be at that trig test, boy, though Hell or high waters try to stop you. Now, tell me, what was this boy's name?"

✧

"O'Connell?" Agnus shouted, to the world in general, after Liam had been sent upstairs to study for his test. "It would be a bleeding O'Connell. They're springing up all over the place this week."

"I believe he's Connor's grandson," said Charlie.

"Ruben's kid, I presume?" Agnus asked.

"Yeah," replied Charlie. "He's a bit of a monster, in looks *and* deed."

"He's a wee s..." Agnus started.

"Now, now, dear," said Charlie, jumping in, "don't get stressed over this."

"How am I not supposed to get stressed?" asked Agnus. "We've only just had Connor giving us grief and here we have the spawn of his spawn causing trouble with my wee cub. Derik aside, I'm getting seriously annoyed with this O'Connell family."

"Derik?" Charlie asked before continuing, "Never mind, it doesn't matter. Don't spend too much of your mind on this. We'll go down to the school, tomorrow and see what the Headmaster has to say for himself."

"I know Liam should never have hit the kid," said Agnus sadly, "but he shouldn't be suspended for it. It's that wee muppet of a grandkid that needs a good whipping."

"Agnus!" Charlie scolded.

"Don't you '*Agnus*' me," she replied. "There're worse things you could do to that boy than a good whipping. Five minutes with a firm cane and he'll soon see the error of his ways."

"You can't do that, these days," said Charlie. "There're laws."

"I'm only joking," Agnus said, "well, half-joking anyway."

"I'm sure, once we talk to the Headmaster, we'll be able to sort it all out," said Charlie.

"We'd better," Agnus replied. "I don't know how much more I can take. These last number of weeks have been pretty tough, for all different reasons."

"Yes, well I'm sure things will start to get better," Charlie said, softly. "You were just after phoning me up to say you've got that engine working."

"We can thank Derik O'Connell for that," Agnus replied. "He's a wee genius with engines."

"There you go, then," Charlie smiled. "Through adversity, you received the exact help you needed at the time."

"Sorry?" Agnus asked, a bit confused.

"I was just saying that, if you never had that confrontation with Connor, then Derik would never have come around to the lockup and your engine would be sitting on blocks right now."

Agnus thought about this. "I suppose you're right," she replied, "but I don't like that our wee Liam's got involved."

"He's not *that* wee anymore," said Charlie. "You should have seen that O'Connell kid. His face was out to here," he held his palm up, a good inch from his own face.

"I still don't like him fighting," Agnus said, strongly. "It's only a matter of time before he comes up against someone stronger and then where will he be?"

"I think that's between him and the priest," Charlie answered.

"This is no time for jokes," Agnus scorned.

"Sorry, love," said Charlie. "I was only trying to lighten the mood."

"It didn't work," said Agnus.

"I can see that," Charlie replied.

They stayed up talking for a while before they took some tea and toast up to bed with them. It had been a long day and Agnus was exhausted. Her mind was full of all that had been going on recently and she was finding it difficult to process it all adequately.

As she dipped her buttered toast, *folded*, into her tea and ate it all, bite by glorious bite, she wondered what else could go wrong for them. It had been a tough old ride for them all and she wasn't sure how many more hits they could cope with. Agnus really hoped that, after they saw the Headmaster in the morning, they would be able to put an end to the situation and move on. The O'Connell family would certainly not be on her Christmas card list.

Chapter 30: The Headmaster

Agnus and Charlie arrived at the school at nine in the morning and walked into the reception area, past the security dogs and through the metal detectors.

"You know," said Charlie, "this school's really changed since I was here."

"From what I heard, you weren't actually here all that much," Agnus replied.

"I got bored," Charlie said. "Never had much of an interest back then. It wasn't until after I left that I realised I would need to find a job."

"Well, you've certainly grown into a fine man," said Agnus, smiling.

"Thanks," Charlie replied. "I do try."

"And you succeed," she replied, lovingly.

The receptionist pressed a button on the desk and a security guard took charge of them, guiding them through the school and on to the Headmaster's office. They were directed into a waiting room and were left to their own devices as they waited to be called through.

As Agnus thanked the guard for his help and closed the door, she got a glimpse of something terrible, mirrored in the glass, and spun around. Sergey and Tarquin were both there in front of her. Sergey was slouching in a chair next to the window. He wore handcuffs and a soulful look as he stared longingly at the outside world. Tarquin, on the other hand, was sitting on the other side of the room, underneath a standing lamp, reading a book on personal relationships and how to build a bridge between the souls. It was a long title so he hoped that it would be sufficiently profound.

Agnus groaned and Charlie quickly put his palm to her back. "Are you alright?" he asked.

"Oh, yes," Agnus replied. "I'm just having a wee moment."

"Are *they* here?" Charlie asked, concerned.

"Yes," Agnus replied, complying with their new rule of complete honesty. "The ass is over there next to the window and the donkey is over there by the lamp."

Sergey and Tarquin both took umbrage at this remark. "Please," said Sergey, "don't be trying to pull us down to your level."

"You can't really be brought down much further than you already are," Agnus replied.

"What did he say?" Charlie asked.

"He's just being all pragmatic," said Agnus. "He's a bit cocky."

"I see," said Charlie, who didn't.

"Going in to see about that kid of yours, are we?" said Sergey, provocatively.

"*We're* not doing anything," said Agnus, getting annoyed already. Sergey had a smile you just wanted to slap off of him. "Me and Charlie here are going in and the two of you can just sod off."

"What did I do?" asked Tarquin, upset. "Here I was, quietly reading my book and I'm put upon by some woman."

"I'll give you '*some woman*'," Agnus yelled. She walked over to Tarquin and slapped him right in the face.

Charlie, who obviously couldn't see the Angel and only saw Agnus swinging in the wind, grabbed her and held her in a bear grip until she stopped wriggling. The anger was still broiling inside her and, with the inability to move her body, she screamed, "Why won't they both just *BUGGER OFF!*"

Agnus realised what she had said as soon as the words had left her lips. This brought her out of her state and when she looked around, tears falling down her face, Sergey and Tarquin were nowhere to be seen. It was just her bad luck that, at the same time as her outburst, the Headmaster's newly qualified personal assistant came walking through the door. She squealed in shock and ran back into the Headmaster's study, slamming the door behind her.

Charlie sat Agnus down on one of the chairs and held her until she stopped crying. He pulled out a clean hankie from his pocket and gave it to Agnus to wipe the tears away.

She felt so daft for letting it get on top of her. She would have thought that she would have gotten used to those two by now. It only goes to show, she thought, small irritations can creep up on you and bite.

She would have to work on her patience and not let problems build up like this. It did her no good and she disliked the thought of losing control of her own mind. Agnus had always been a strong, formidable woman and the idea that this would not always be the case made her scared beyond belief. She could lose everything but not her mind. Her mind was who she was and if that went then who would she be?

This and many other thoughts plagued her. She was only brought out of it when the young assistant edged back into the waiting room, squeaked that the Headmaster would see them now and went running back out of the room through the door to the hallway.

Agnus and Charlie stood up and walked through the door to the Headmaster's study. When inside, they saw that every spare wall space had been filled with very fine, handcrafted, bookshelves. A great number of books filled the space therein. His desk was an original partner desk and sat under the window, looking into the room. This room belonged to a man who loved to read and write.

The Headmaster stood up to greet them and directed the couple towards two chairs in front of the desk. Agnus and Charlie sat there, Agnus' cheeks burning with shame. She was distraught about what had happened, especially about that girl coming in when she did and didn't know how she could go about explaining the situation.

She sat there, nervously playing with her watch, while the Headmaster moved some papers off of his desk and pulled out Liam's case file.

"First of all," said the Headmaster, "I want you to know that you don't have to worry about before. I am aware of your current health problems and I personally have experience of the matter, so I do understand the problems."

Agnus sighed, in gratitude, relaxing a bit. Then she had a thought. "Experience?" she asked.

"My mother," the Headmaster replied. "She was pretty far gone by the end."

"I'm sorry to hear that," said Agnus.

"It's been twelve years now, since she passed and it was more of a blessing when her time came, in her eyes at least."

Agnus didn't like the sound of that possible future.

"But we didn't come here to talk about Mother," the Headmaster continued. "I must say that I'm sorry things have come to this point. Liam is a good kid and studious but we cannot allow fights to break out in the middle of the playground."

"He was only protecting his mother's honour," said Charlie. "That's got to count for something."

"Liam refuses to comment on the situation," the Headmaster continued. "If he spoke to me and explained himself then I might be able to go easier on him but he's remaining irritatingly quiet on the subject."

"The other boys, particularly this O'Connell kid, were teasing Liam, telling him that his mother was going to die."

"That's unacceptable behaviour, here," said the Headmaster, stunned at the depths kids were willing to go. "I shall, of course, deal with it promptly. However, if I had known all this before, I would not have been so heavy handed."

Agnus sighed again, in relief.

"I cannot condone the fighting, however," the Headmaster went on. "I will lift his suspension but he will have to do an hour a day after class, in the school's new botanic nursery, for three weeks."

"I think we can deal with that," said Charlie. "What do you think, Agnus?"

"I think that's fair," Agnus replied. "When can he come back to school?"

"Tomorrow, if he's able," said the Headmaster.

"Oh, he will be," replied Agnus, "or else."

Agnus left the school, hand-in-hand with Charlie, a little less stress on her shoulders than when she had entered. It didn't give her a good feeling to have so much association with this O'Connell family but, one problem sorted, she put it to the back of her mind.

Chapter 31: The Check-up

The next day, Charlie had Agnus down the hospital clinic to see the inquisitive Dr. Ashcroft. They sat in the second waiting room of the day and waited to be called. Agnus was so relieved, when the nurse came in to call her name, that Sergey and Tarquin had failed to turn up.

They followed the nurse down the hall, once again, and entered the doctor's office when their knock was answered. Inside, they sat right down and Dr. Ashcroft asked them the age old question.

"So, how have you been keeping?" the doctor asked.

"Not too great," said Charlie. "She's had a couple of turns, recently."

"Ok, then," the doctor replied, flicking through her notes.

She then went on to do a battery of tests. Eyes, ears, throat, balance, blood pressure, height and weight, they were all put through their paces. Agnus felt very uncomfortable throughout the whole ordeal and when the mad doctor brought out a device for measuring the size of her head she told Dr. Ashcroft that she was through.

"The shape or size of my head has nothing to do with my illness," said Agnus, firmly.

"We can never be sure what might give us some light on your problems," Dr. Ashcroft argued, keenly.

"Maybe," said Agnus, "but I think we're past the days of all… *this*," she indicated the device which Dr. Ashcroft was lovingly stroking.

"Oh, would you look at that," said Charlie, suddenly, "I think that's our time." He took Agnus' hand and pulled her out of the doctor's office and down the corridor. "Bleeding witchdoctor," he said as they marched down the corridors. "We're just as well figuring this out ourselves. We'll go see Dr. Cameron tomorrow and see what he can give you for these issues."

"She wasn't all that bad," said Agnus.

"She's a couple of test tubes short of a chemistry set," Charlie replied. "Madder than a bag of spanners."

"How can a bag of spanners be mad?" Agnus asked.

"What?" asked Charlie, paused in his rant by a sudden change in mental direction. "I don't know. It's just a saying."

"I'm not sure it is," Agnus replied. "It sounds like you're the one who's getting confused." She smiled, lovingly.

Charlie paused again, saw her smile and returned it, relaxing. "I just don't want you being looked after by some hack," said Charlie.

"I know," Agnus replied. "We'll go see Dr. Cameron tomorrow."

They drove home, less tense but still concerned for the future. It was going to be a long and tough stretch but they had each other and that was important to remember. Agnus was going to make the most of her time and as soon as this race was over, next week, they would be making the most of every free moment together before it was too late.

When they got home, Agnus made the point of cooking dinner herself. She wanted to get things back to a state of normality. It was important for them to have structure during this time. They needed that stability in order to cope with the future.

Agnus' heart broke every time she thought about it. The problems she was having at the moment; the stiff bones; the pains and the headaches; even the hallucinations were only the start of things. This was not something that could be cured or even really controlled. She would have to deal with the issues as they occurred and, for the rest of her natural life, they would only get worse.

The stress and pain that she was going to bring on Charlie and Liam hurt Agnus to her very soul. It was going to be terrible for the both of them to watch her deteriorate and become a fraction of the woman she was at the present. It would place them under a great deal of pressure physically and mentally and Agnus wished she could spare them from it all.

She couldn't take that way out, though. It would hurt Charlie and Liam more to go down that route. She couldn't do that to them and there was, of course, the issue of her immortal soul. It was a terrible sin to take your own life and she didn't want to end up *down there*, with people worse than Sergey when she had just escaped the prison of her illness. It was all a matter of belief, of course, and as a stout protestant, she had hers.

After dinner, Agnus watched the recording of her show while sipping a cup of tea. She still missed her green mug. All the other mugs were fine enough but that one had been hers. Nobody else used it and it always felt better to drink out of that one than any of the others, simply because it was hers.

She watched as Bradley directed the contestants through the game and even laughed occasionally as the giggling presenter came up against his Achilles heel; his old friend, the innuendo. He was a loveable character and she smiled every time she saw his puppy face. She decided that this was what she needed to have more of in her life. It was important to have goals but it was also just as important to have rest and a time just to relax and smile.

Agnus went to bed, that night, stilled but also nervous for the future. The fact that they only had one week left till the race was also something that was on her mind. It was a blessing to get the engine fixed when they did. Derik would always have a place in her heart for that, the poor soul.

There was still the last of the wee jobs to do before getting the paintwork done. The girls had all agreed that it would only be right that they present the Beeline logo on the car and also Tommy's garage who had helped them with parts and tyres as they went on this journey. A design had been decided upon, so all they needed to do was get the lads down to spray it and lay the logos in place.

It was an exciting time and Agnus really hoped that they hadn't forgotten anything important. Tommy was on the ball, though. He was making sure that all the boxes were ticked when they needed to be. Yes, everything would be fine, from here on in. The excitement built up inside Agnus and, unfortunately, caused her to have difficulty dropping off to sleep. Drifting in and out all night, Agnus had dreams of cars, mud and champagne. She really hoped it was a premonition.

Chapter 32: The Lost Sheep

When Agnus arrived at the lockup, the next morning, it was to the news that the car was complete apart from the paintwork. Derik's handiwork was impeccable and the engine had started the very first time, causing delight in all present. The girls had worked especially hard the previous day and were still there at two in the morning, finishing up.

The pleasure that Agnus felt to walk around the finished car was ecstatic. She ran her hand across the roof and down the frame to the bonnet. It was perfect.

"I know it still doesn't look like much," said Lilly, "but she's a cracker. She'll actually be able to give some of the other cars a run for their money."

"Good," said Agnus, "I want to make a mark."

The other girls looked at each other, slightly worried at this remark.

Agnus looked up and saw them staring at her. "Don't worry," she said, "I'm not going mental, or anything. I just want us to do well, what with all the troubles we've had in getting here. This should be an amazing experience for us all. It should be *memorable*."

"It will be," said Eva. "The car's ready for you. All that needs doing now is ready up for the race."

"We're going to do this," said Agnus, with a focused look, "and we're going to do well."

They decided to take the day and spend some time getting the lockup back into a reasonable state. With all the work they had been doing in there over the last while, it had got a bit messy and a lot mucky. There were tools, cloths and oil everywhere and since they had completed the car, they figured they should really tidy up the midden they had created around them.

At around ten am, there was a colossal roar of an engine coming from outside. It gained in volume and then stopped suddenly when it, *whatever it was*, got close to them. As they stood in their still positions, the doors burst open and in stormed Connor.

He was steaming at the ears and his gaze was darting about the lockup, searching everywhere that was visible. "Where is he," Connor demanded.

"Listen here, Mr. O'Connell," said Agnus. "I don't know where you were brought up but here, it is not polite to just burst into somebody's workspace and make demands."

"I'll have none of your nonsense," said Connor. "Just tell me where that useless lump of a boy is and I'll be on my way."

"For your information," said Agnus, sternly, "we have no idea where your poor son is. Even if we did, I think it doubtful that we'd tell you."

"Do you, now," Connor replied. "You don't have your bodyguard with you this time."

"Maybe not," Agnus went on, regardless, "but I'm sure he'd soon find out."

"Not if there was nobody left to tell the tale," Connor replied, grinning an evil smile.

"I think he'd put two and two together, all the same," said Agnus. "He's a bright boy, that one."

"Look, I've got no time for your banter today," said Connor, irritated and angry; a bad combination. "I just want to find my boy and take him home. Where… is… he?" he finished through gritted teeth.

"I told you," said Agnus. "we don't know. Now, I would appreciate it if you could just leave."

"I don't believe you," said Connor. "The last place he was heading was here. Two witnesses saw him come down here."

"I don't know what else to tell you," said Agnus, patiently, "but he's not here now and I have no clue where he could be."

Connor looked exasperated and still angry but he was coming to the realisation that this was going nowhere.

"I'll find him," he said, as a lame sort of threat.

"Very good," Agnus replied, simply.

Connor made to storm off, theatrically but failed to spot a lead pipe lying on the floor. He went base over apex and landed flat on his back, the wind knocked out of him. The girls rushed over to help him but he refused emphatically, pushing them away when they came close. He pulled himself up off of the floor and limped over to and through the doors which he had originally burst through and drove away.

The girls all agreed that it had been a surprising event but something they should have expected. Their hand in the disappearance of Derik was all too clear to them and they felt that they really ought to have seen this coming. From what they had seen before this day, Connor wasn't the nicest of people and he was bound to come a calling when his youngest son went missing.

For the rest of the morning, they continued in their cleaning and by the time lunch came, the place was more sparkly than ever it had been. There were obviously a great many oil marks that couldn't be removed but that being said they had done a remarkable job.

They had a nice lunch outside of sandwiches and wine and enjoyed the feeling of a job well done, any and all thoughts of Connor and his family gone from their minds. It was a pleasant time and each of the girls were glad to have some time of peace in each other's company. The car was complete, except for the paintwork, and the lockup was spanky again. The whole shebang was pristine and they felt a real sense of accomplishment as they looked upon their efforts. Everything was shiny.

Just as they were about to tidy away their lunch apparatus, they saw Tommy's car coming down the path. They could see that he had someone in the passenger side of the car with him. When they had pulled up and exited the vehicle, they wandered over to the girls and they managed to get a good look at the young man. Young was the right word, too.

"Tommy," Lilly asked, slowly, "why have you brought a child here, with you? Is there something you need to tell me?"

"This is Billy," said Tommy. "He may only be sixteen but he's the best sprayer in the business. A right wee artiste."

"Don't you mean *artist?*" asked Big May.

"No," Tommy replied. "He's very clear that he's an *artiste.*"

"Fair enough," said Agnus, "and he's going to paint the car, then?"

"Indeed," Tommy said. "He's the bomb."

"Don't say that," said Billy, sighing. "You can't do it right."

Tommy looked a little downhearted at this knockdown but quickly pulled himself together. "He's seen the designs and had made a couple of improvements. That's what we're calling them isn't it?" he asked Billy.

"Definitely," Billy replied.

"Good, good," said Agnus, who had a slight doubt in her mind and had a feeling that this might all go horribly wrong.

They showed Billy the car and he retrieved his bag of goodies from Tommy's back seat. He walked around the car for a while, looking at it from every angle and doing some kind of calculations in his head. He then looked at the designs for a while, holding them up to the relative parts of the vehicle. It wasn't until he did all that, that he opened up his bag and started pulling out a whole range of different spray cans. There were at least five different shades of blue, three of green and, to Agnus' astonishment, seven shades of yellow. Other colours were there in the mix as well and the full count looked rather like around twenty-five cans, of one tint or another.

 Billy, although very young, obviously took his work seriously and it was another fifteen minutes of close inspections and selections before he picked up his first can and started the base coat. Agnus and the girls decided to go home for the day and let them get on with it. They would come back on the morning of the showing, to see the car in all its glory. If Tommy's excitement was anything to go by, they were in for something special.

 All in all, they were happy with their day. The small altercation with Connor aside, everything had been good. Car done, lock-up clean and the car was being sprayed as they got the bus home. Yes, it had been a good day and they were all feeling bright and breezy with the excitement of the race coming up. There were only a few more days to go and a thrill was beginning to come over them as they imagined what it would be like.

 Agnus watched her show in the evening, as was usual after her dinner. She realised that with all the anticipation, it was hard to concentrate on the questions and she lost track a couple of times. Nevertheless, she enjoyed her time in front of the television, only missing her mug once or twice. To put it simply, Agnus was quite content. She was starting to get a handle on life and it even looked like they had a real chance of turning some heads at this race.

Agnus slept well that night with all her dreams being happy ones.

Chapter 33: The Congratulatory Dinner

The next evening, the girls were all asked to meet Tommy down at the lockup and told to wear something nice. This puzzled the girls. There was nothing else, that they could think of, that they needed to do down there. Why they should wear something nice was also confusing. Maybe there was someone from the rally coming to see the car or something.

Agnus made herself up and selected a skirt and blouse that she normally kept for good. When she came down from her room, after she was ready, it was to the sound of a wolf-whistle from Charlie and a "Wow," from Liam.

"I take it I look alright, then," said Agnus.

"You're perfect," Charlie replied.

Agnus blushed. They had been married for ten years now but it was nice to know that Charlie was still willing to make the effort. She did feel quite grand in her good clothes. It was nice to be able to dress up of an evening and enjoy it.

Charlie said that he'd give her a lift but there was somewhere he had to be. Agnus said that it was alright. She wanted everyone in town to see her all dressed up, to make a showing of going out. It was her way of telling the world, *I'm doing fine. Nothing wrong here.*

The girls met at the bus stop, all of them in their finest clothes. They all looked the belle of the ball, standing there in the middle of the council estate. They got a few calls of, "*Your Majesties,*" from the local kids but the girls just ignored them and they moved on by when they got bored.

When they arrived at the lockup, it was bolted from the inside.

"What's going on?" Eva asked.

"Not sure," Agnus replied. "I can hear voices."

"Yes, but that's not a strange thing for you," said Eva. She got a slap on the back of the head from Big May. "I was only kidding," she cried.

"Does anyone else get the feeling something's wrong here?" Big May inquired, still giving Eva a rough look of disapproval.

"I'm sure that if Tommy asked us to come down here, he must have a reason," said Lilly, protectively. "I'm sure everything's fine. Try knocking."

Big May banged her heavy fist on the door three times and they waited for an answer.

After a few seconds, the bolt was slid back and Tommy popped his head out and slid himself through the door, making sure the girls didn't see what was going on inside.

"What's happening?" Big May demanded.

"Is there something wrong with the car?" Eva asked.

"Just tell us," said Lilly, "come on."

"Girls, girls," said Tommy smiling, "please relax. There's nothing wrong with the car. In fact, she's running like a dream and looking even better."

"So, what's going on?" Agnus asked. "Why have you brought us down here and why won't you let us see inside?"

"Girls," said Tommy, "you've all been through a lot over the last couple of months and you've worked your hardest, throughout it all. We just thought you deserved a little celebration before you start the race itself."

Tommy chose this moment to open the doors wide and present the girls with a view that astounded them and lifted their hearts. In the middle of the room was a large circular table with ten seats around it. It was set for dinner and looked like you would see in the finest of restaurants. The tablecloth was white but a strip of tartan cloth went down the centre of the table, to add a bit of colour. A candelabrum sat in the centre which really set things off. Even the napkins were folded into little waiter's jackets, each with a small purple thistle attached as a make-shift button hole.

What was even better was that, behind the table, were all the people who had held them together, through the whole project. There were Tommy and Terry; Billy and John; as well as Jack and Jim, Eva and Big May's husbands. Everyone was there and it filled their hearts with joy to see them all.

Tommy took the girls' coats and they all sat down around the table. The girls were amazed to see that, not only had they put this dinner on for them but they had gone to the effort of hiring a team of proper waiters and waitresses to serve. It was like being in a real restaurant.

When the starters came, it was an elaborate prawn cocktail. Agnus thought it looked almost too good to eat. *Almost*. She scoffed it down, as did the others and it tasted just as good as it had looked. Everyone chatted and laughed and enjoyed their time together.

Waitresses came around with white wine. It was a lovely Italian pinot grigio and the girls were impressed with the selection. It was a sweet wine with a light kick. They had finished two bottles before they knew it and more had to be sent for.

"It's fine," said Tommy, "we've got plenty chilled in the back."

The main course was a beautiful fillet of cod with an orange and lemon sauce. It was incredibly prepared and the plate was like a work of art. How the chef managed to cook this kind of a meal on these premises was beyond Agnus' comprehension but she took her hat off to him or her.

They had a wonderful time, having a relaxed dinner. It was nice to cool down and enjoy themselves without one of them ending up in the jail or the hospital. They had all put so much into this project of theirs and they more than deserved to have an evening of light-heartedness and fun. This evening more than did that. It was a blessed time and Agnus enjoyed every minute of it.

Desert came and the girls were, once again, wowed into silence. Once the mains had been cleared away, they were presented with an enormous and very appetising lemon meringue pie. It was delicious and melted on the tongue. Never before had they tasted such luxurious flavours. The whole meal had been fantastic and this really finished it off to a tee.

Things didn't finish there, however. After desert, they were served with tea and/or coffee and some small black slates were placed on the table which contained ten pieces of soft white chocolate fudge. This too was glorious. It was the softest fudge in the world and the tongue begged for more before the first piece was finished being swallowed.

As they were discussing the sweetness of the fudge, a trolley was wheeled in with a huge cake on top. It was, unsurprisingly, in the shape of a 1999 Ford Escort and had frosting similar to the colours on Misses Ford.

"It's perfection itself," said Agnus who was overawed by the whole evening.

Agnus then gave a small speech about love and hard work and all the things and people she was grateful for. It ended in tears but they were happy ones, so it was all good. Lilly then got up and made a speech of her own, thanking Agnus for getting them into this in the first place. They were well aware that this was all Agnus' dream but they felt, in a way, that it was theirs too.

Agnus had replied that yes, it was all of theirs and the work they put into the car was proof of that. She went on to say that she would hold them all close to her heart, forever and she really couldn't thank them enough.

They all went home that evening, happy and full. It was a great evening, enjoyed by all and they all wished that they could do it more often. They each went back to their own homes, by way of a fleet of taxis and took to their beds, drowsy from all the wine.

Happy dreams were had by all.

Chapter 34: The Spit and Polish

Agnus and Charlie both awoke feeling a bit rough but it was a happy kind of rough. They took their time in rising and when they got downstairs they found that Liam, who had predicted their tenderness, had ordered in what he considered to be the ultimate hangover cure, pizza and irn-bru.

They wolfed this down and found that it was, surprisingly enough, what their bodies needed. They had a cup of tea afterwards, to finish it all off, and sat at the kitchen table, chatting away till Charlie noticed that it was gone midday and Agnus was due to be down at the lockup for final inspection before they displayed Misses Ford, the next day.

Agnus got herself ready while Charlie helped Liam tidy up after brunch. She threw on her work togs and trotted downstairs again, pulling on her coat and hat. Saying goodbye to Liam and thanking him for brunch, Agnus and Charlie left the house and made their way down to the lockup in Charlie's car.

The journey was uneventful and they made it there in good time. Charlie went off again, saying he'd pick Agnus, Eva and Big May up later on when they were ready to come home. Agnus smiled happily as she waved him goodbye. She loved that man so much. She couldn't have made it through all this without him by her side the whole time, even when she didn't know it or believe it.

Agnus entered the lockup and greeted her friends. The girls were there, as were Tommy and Terry. There were also three cars, instead of just Misses Ford. The first new car was the one that Agnus had been driving up at the racing track. The only difference now was that it looked the part. Gone were the dents and missing body parts. This was a spanky car now and, she was informed, had had a real boost on the internal front.

The thing could go like the clappers and had great power of acceleration.

    The third car in the room was something different indeed. It was a dark red, Dodge Charger with two white stripes running down the centre of the bonnet[10], roof and boot[11].

    Tommy said that it was a 2.7 litre V8 with more power than your average entrant. It looked the part, too. If you looked at it straight on, you could almost swear that it was growling. It was a beast of a car, right enough and Agnus thought it was a fine addition to the team.

    Their final day was spent waxing and polishing the three impressive vehicles. They took their time and a lot of care, making sure to check for dirt or small stones on the cloth before they placed it anywhere near the paintwork. It was an enjoyable time for them all. There was no stress and everyone went around with a smile on their face, happy in the work they had all done and delighted that they had actually made it to this stage. They were there, they were ready and they were going to give it all they had.

    The only time they stopped, apart from lunch at midday, was when there was a knock on the door and a nervous and spotty youth crept into the lockup, carrying a big presentation tube. Agnus wondered what was inside it.

    They called the boy in and he entered, with some trepidation. "Er," he said, "I… I've got a… a delivery for an… Aganus?"

    "You tell us," said Eva. "You're the one with the card."

    Agnus stepped forward. "*I'm Aganus,*" she said in a strong and bold voice.

---

[10] The hood
[11] The trunk

"Why can't you just tell him it's spelt wrongly," sighed Lilly. "We don't need the dramatics."

The boy was standing there, at (sort of) attention. He had his knees together and appeared to be shifting his weight from one foot to the other. Agnus looked at his face and saw nothing but the purest concentration. By the looks of things what _he_ needed now, more than anything else in the world, was a bathroom.

"It's the door behind the Dodge," said Agnus, to the utter delight of the young man. He nodded in appreciation and waddled off as carefully as he could, handing the big cardboard tube to Agnus.

"What is it, do you wonder?" asked Eva.

"Let her open the bleeding thing," said Big May.

Agnus placed the tube, which was marked with a 'this way up' sticker, on the table and cracked open the plastic stickers which held the lid on. Pulling off said lid, Agnus looked inside and gasped.

"What is it?" asked Eva.

Agnus reached into the tube, got a hold of the item and slowly pulled it out. The proper term should really be *pulled them out* because it was, in fact, a bunch of flowers, roses no less. The only thing that was odd about them was the colour. Instead of being the usual red or white, this bunch of twelve was, in their entirety apart from the stems, *black*.

"That's a bit dark," said Big May.

"Yeah," added a shocked Eva, "I've never been sent black roses before."

"Who does it say it's from?" Lilly asked, curious as ever.

Agnus searched around for a card. She eventually found it in amongst the flowers themselves. She removed her glasses and looked at the writing on the card. There was only one word there. There only needed to be one. Any more would have been a tautology.

"Well?" asked Eva, "What does it say?"

"*O'Connell*," said Agnus, simply

Tommy told the girls not to worry about it and that it was just Connor's sick way of trying to psyche them out. Agnus and the girls weren't all that sure they believed him. In their minds, if someone sent you a bunch of black roses, it meant that they wanted you dead. This gave Agnus some fears for the race. If Connor wanted her dead and they came up against each other during the race, what he might try was greatly disturbing.

Tommy and Terry tried to talk the girls down and, after a great deal of time and shouting, they managed it and they all sat around the cars, quietly staring at the floor.

"So, what do we do?" asked Eva.

"We do nothing," said Tommy. "They're just a bunch of scaremongers. They wouldn't actually harm you on purpose."

"What about accidents?" asked Big May.

"There won't be any *accidents*" Tommy replied. "We'll be keeping a watchful eye on things as a precautionary measure."

"If everything's fine, then why do we need precautionary measures?" Lilly asked, firmly.

"Look," said Tommy, getting exasperated, "everything will be fine. There is no need to worry. The O'Connell's are harmless. They just look like vicious thugs and that's how they work. They put on a hard face but they run as soon as they're in a situation that's even a little hot."

"I just don't like the idea of some brute coming after my friend," said Lilly.

"And anyway," said Terry, "he knows well enough that if he tries anything on you girls, anything at all, then John will take personal umbrage and he'll be banned from the race along with his philistine of a son."

Agnus reckoned this was probably true and the words helped her relax slightly. She just hoped that Connor wasn't so riled by the girls' efforts and disrespect that he'd forget about being sanctioned and let his urges have free reign.

Chapter 35: The Weigh-in

Agnus got up, on the day they were to present Misses Ford to the public, feeling refreshed but also anxious and in two minds about whether to go or to slip back into bed and spend the day hugging her duvet.

She expelled the thought too late.

"Hello," said Tarquin, as Agnus was rinsing her mouth, post-brushing.

"Come off it," Agnus sighed. "Why? And where's that pal of yours?"

A head popped out from behind the shower curtain where she could hear water running. "Hey," said Sergey, who had a clear plastic shower hat on his head, "this is some good water pressure, you have here." From what Agnus could see, the shower hat was all he was wearing.

"Hay is for horses," said Agnus, automatically, trying to remember what she should be doing next in order to get ready. Most of her brainpower, however, was spent on attempting to ignore her two afflictions.

"You know," said Sergey, from behind the curtain, "there's nothing wrong with being concerned for your safety."

"She'll be fine," replied Tarquin. "Tommy did say that Connor's bark was worse than his bite and, as for the race itself, Agnus has become a pretty decent driver."

"Pretty decent?" asked Agnus. "I think I'm a little better than, *pretty decent*."

"I could beat you in a broken down milk truck," said Sergey.

"Well," Agnus replied, "then I say it's a good thing you're not in the race, then."

Sergey sulked and slipped behind the curtain again.

Agnus looked at herself in the mirror. Tarquin had a point. Connor was unlikely to try anything during the race. He wants the prize more than a confrontation with the girls. The flowers were just him saying that he was going to leave them in his dust as he raced towards the finish line. Agnus wasn't going to make it that easy and, in that moment, she decided to put her best foot forward and go into this with all she had. Agnus took a deep breath, straightened her back and brought back her shoulders. "Let's do this," she said to herself.

*

Agnus, Charlie and Liam arrived at the race in Charlie's car which pulled his and Liam's entry on a trailer. Their other two friends were going to be arriving later with their specific cars but Charlie wanted to be at the side of the loch where the showing would take place, to help Agnus find her way about. He didn't like the idea of her wandering about by herself.

They parked up and walked through the swarms of people already at the lochside. The place was buzzing with excitement and flash cars. Agnus loved to see what the other driving teams had brought to offer. She really wished that she could see what was under their bonnets.

"That's what the showing is all about," said Charlie, as they passed a blue Subaru Impreza with gold wheel rims. "They have all the cars lined up with their bonnets open, for the whole world to see. There's a chain running along, mind, to stop anyone fiddling with anything and you stand next to it looking all cool and spunky."

Agnus, although considered a tough broad, was not one to put herself forward. The thought of everyone staring at her as she stood beside Misses Ford, with nothing to do but twiddle her thumbs, made her a little nervous. She hoped it wouldn't take long.

They found where the rest of the girls were camped up and joined them. Big May had acquired a camper van from somewhere and they had set up a barbeque for the making of breakfast rolls. There was a wonderful aroma coming from the bacon and square sausage as it cooked on the grill. The smell alone could fill you up.

As they munched on their hot rolls and discussed the day, Tommy and Terry came walking up to the group, smiling with excitement. They were duly passed a couple of rolls each and then asked about the day's proceedings. Charlie said that this was his and Liam's cue to leave and they finished up and went on back to their own project.

Once they were alone, the day was discussed in length. Everyone wanted to make sure that they didn't miss anything or, even worse, do something wrong.

✲

The day began at one pm with the sponsors putting on a short music show with local bands. It was very elaborate and very loud. Agnus fancied they could hear it all the way over on the other side of the loch.

After that, the hired host of the weekend's events showed face and welcomed everyone to the day's events. He made some jokes that might have been funny if Agnus had understood them and left the stage, inviting everyone to join him, half an hour later, for the showing of the cars.

This was the signal for the girls, Tommy and Terry to find their vehicle of choice and drive it over to the presentation area and park it in the position that they had been informed of previously. Their cars all being parked in a line beside each other, Agnus stood there beside Tommy and Terry, smiling and trying not to let the bustling crowd overwhelm her.

When Agnus got used to the crowds of people, she started to enjoy herself. There were a great many people interested in what Misses Ford had under the bonnet. They were also, Agnus discovered, very interested in her and the stories they had all been hearing about four grannies building a car[12]. She also saw Liam, nine cars up, smiling like Tony Blair on a pre-election tour.

For some reason, the girls had become the toast of the town and they had no idea that it was happening. People were talking about *them* and were genuinely interested in their story. There were even a couple of journalists who were looking for a quote for *their own* story.

All in all, Agnus enjoyed her experience in the public eye. It had not been as bad as she had expected and it was a load off of her mind, more so when she was allowed to leave. Driving Misses Ford away from the display area, she followed Tommy and Terry to where they were to store the cars overnight before the race.

Terry had said that he had doubts about security and so he had brought a huge lorry with him to make it possible to put the cars behind lock and chain. They placed the vehicles in the lorry and locked it up tight for the night.

The truck was then left in the charge of two big and multi-scarred men who looked like they would eat you. The girls found out very quickly that Boltcutter and Knuckles were two of the nicest guys in the world. They said that they would take very good care of the cars for the girls and to rest their little minds. The girls liked these lads, so decided to let that

---

[12] She tried to explain that none of them was in fact a grandmother but it fell on deaf ears.

particular comment fly past. With Boltcutter and Knuckles in charge of the lorry, there was not a soul who would dare try to tamper with it.

This made Agnus feel at ease about leaving the cars in the parking area. They were going to be spending the night in a campervan that Charlie had the forethought to hire. There was space for all three of them and even a lounge area where they could have a nice meal before they went to their beds.

It had been a great day and gave promise for the race itself. Agnus went to sleep that night with happy thoughts and her loved ones around her.

Five hundred yards away, Boltcutter and Knuckles stood at ease at the rear of the lorry, their hands clasped in front of them. They would sleep in the morning. For now, they had a job to do and they'd be blown if they weren't going to do it right.

Chapter 36: The Morning Of

In the morning, Agnus woke to the smell of bacon frying in the next room. She got out of the camper's bed slipped into her dressing gown and opened the not very robust door. Walking through to the lounge area, Agnus saw that Charlie and Liam were already up, dressed and sitting at the small table, eating a full fry up of sausage, bacon, eggs, mushrooms, fried bread, potato scones, hash browns, baked beans, pork chops and fried potatoes with buttered toast on the side.

"It's the breakfast of champions," said Charlie as a mild excuse. "I've left you some in the pan. It'll do you good to get something solid inside you."

Agnus looked in the pan at a sausage that had been burnt black. "Solid is the right word," she said, poking it with a fork.

They had their breakfast and got ready for the day. Agnus dressed in her racing gear, as did Liam, and they marched out in their respective directions to meet up with their separate teams. As Agnus walked the short distance to Big May's camper van, she was amazed at the number of people who had joined them beside the loch. Agnus had thought that there had been a lot of people on the previous day but the population of the grounds had risen by at least two hundred percent and it was crazy. Agnus squeezed her way through the swarms of drivers, mechanics, event organisers and, overwhelming them all, the thousand-person-strong crowd.

She eventually found her way through the jostle and wandered over to where the girls, Tommy and Terry were sitting around, drinking tea out of tin cups. Agnus' teeth itched at the sight of it. Luckily she had a normal mug in her handbag which would do the trick. It wasn't her green one but she would cope.

Big May poured some tea into Agnus' mug and they conversed for a while. They were all beyond excited. The whole atmosphere of the lochside was energetic and their hearts were all going at sixteen to the dozen, adrenaline rushing through their bodies at the thought of what was to come throughout the day.

Once they had all finished gossiping, they packed up their things into the camper van and made their way to the lorry. When they got there, Boltcutter and Knuckles were still standing in the same positions as they had been when Agnus and the boys had left them the night before. Agnus inquired if they had eaten and Boltcutter winked, saying that his wee brother had brought them supplies a couple of times through the night.

"Don't you worry, Mother[13]," he finished, "we didn't starve."

Knuckles opened up the lorry and they reversed the cars out, very carefully to make sure they didn't get a single scratch on their beautiful machines. Agnus was still amazed at how professional they looked and said so to the boys. Tommy replied, saying that it was no less than they deserved, what with all the work the girls had put into it. Not to mention the other troubles they had all had separately while on this journey.

They drove the cars over to where they would enter the starting area, later on that day. There, they opened up the front of all three cars and went through the whole engine, just in case they missed something or a piece got loose during the last couple of days. Agnus enjoyed this time. It was good to have a slow build up to a race that would take it out of them all.

---

[13] A term of respect

Twenty-four hours is a long time and, even though they would be splitting up the driving, it was going to be a tough one. Agnus was glad to have the chill-out time before hand. She found it was quite relaxing, working on the car in the mid-morning warmth of the lochside.

What Agnus didn't realise was that the other girls had plans of their own while she was working on the car. They had found a young girl who was doing face painting and had come up with an idea that they thought was inspired and absolutely hilarious.

The first Agnus knew about it was when she heard a loud shout from the other side of the car and looked up to see her three friends marching towards her, their faces covered in paint.

"You look like Mel Gibson," Agnus said to Eva.

"Who would that make me, then?" asked Big May, perturbed. She had wanted to be Mel.

"Brendon Gleeson," said Lilly, cruelly.

"I'm not that big," said Big May. "Who'd you be then, smarty-pants?"

"The mad Irishman, of course," Lilly replied grinning.

"That's a good one," said Agnus, "everyone loves a mad Irishman, well, most of them," she added, remembering Connor.

"Sure, didn't the Lord send us to watch your back, so," Lilly said, slipping into an Irish lilt.

"Well, I'm glad you're getting into the spirit of the thing," said Tommy, coming over from his own car to congratulate the girls on their war paint. "This event's all about having fun… and the race, of course, but there's a lot more going on here today than just that."

"We saw," said Eva. "They've got a bouncy castle back there where the glade opens and there are a whole load of ice cream vans and hot food stalls."

"There'll be over ten thousand people by the start of the race," said Tommy. "Before all that, there are, as you say, plenty of places to get a bite to eat. There are also a few bands performing and the Edinburgh Society of Street Performers will be wandering around the area, randomly."

"I did see someone breathing fire out of his…" Big May started.

"Never mind where he was blowing it out of," said Lilly. "I did like the jugglers, though."

"That's all lovely," said Agnus. "I'm glad you're all having a good time. I'd better get back to this car, though. Make sure everything's good."

"No problem," said Eva. "We'll go and grab some food and find a spot to watch the entrance parade."

They wandered off in the direction of the cooked meat that wafted through along the lochside. They had heard on the grapevine that there was a man selling ostrich burgers. This was something the girls had never heard of before and they wanted to give it a try.

Agnus carried on checking the car, inside and out before moving across and having a word with Tommy and Terry about the route they had to take. It was a relatively simple path, but there were a few turns that Terry was most insistent that she took at a low speed.

"If you take it too fast," he had said, "you'll end up doing a sideways summersault and go flying off the track. If that happens, the race is over for you. You won't be able to get it flipped back over and back onto the track before your courtesy time is over."

Agnus decided that she really should follow his instructions on this. She was well aware that this would not be the same as driving up at the Beeline racing track. It would be a lot more slippy with all the mud around and there was always the chance of sharp stones that could pop a tyre. They had plenty of new tires sitting in the centre of the track and a couple of Terry's mechanics[14] were there waiting to hop into action if necessary.

Everything was looking good, so long as Agnus didn't get too excited and throw herself off of the track. She needed to stay calm and not to worry about being overtaken. If she kept on the track and stayed at a relative speed for each corner (they had predefined these) she should be fine. Terry had warned her to watch out for other drivers who wished to play bumpers.

"Take your foot off of the accelerator," he had said, "then knock his back wheel and, as he starts to slide, push forward and shove his back end around. He'll end up facing the other way and you can just move on and not have to worry about him again."

Tommy thought this was a bit of a complicated move for Agnus to try but Terry was adamant that she was up to the task, so long as she concentrated and didn't let the car get away from her.

When they had, all three of them, finished what they needed to do with their cars, they stood near the main gate and waited for their cue to start the entrance parade. It was going to be a long twenty-four hours and they appreciated these last few minute of calm before the storm finally hit.

---

[14] or *'Mech-heads'*, as he referred to them

Chapter 37: The Entrance

The drivers lined up from the starting gates. They were all dressed up in their safety clothes and, most of them, had their helmets sitting on top of their respective vehicles. It was quite a sight and Agnus couldn't resist taking a few photographs to remember it by.

As she went to take her final photo, however, she caught a glimpse of Connor and his son, standing by their trio of bright yellow Vauxhall Corsa's. All three were identical apart from the colour of stripe that crossed their roof and bonnet. Thankfully, Connor was too busy making sure his drivers were doing what they were supposed to do and he never noticed Agnus, seven car lengths behind him.

Agnus looked to see Liam but, with the number of drivers here, it was not a surprise that he blended in.

The five-minute warning horn went off and all the drivers involved took to their vehicles, wishing each other good luck, and fastened themselves in. The race itself would begin in a little over half an hour. For now, they would all drive onto the track, in one long line of cars, and take a lap around the course. On seeing the mud soaked mess of a road, Agnus realised *why* it was known more commonly as a course and not a track.

When the horn went off again, every engine started in unison, apart from a couple of vehicles which had ignition problems already. Maybe, once they got them going, they might be ok to race but Agnus doubted they would last very long.

The first car moved off and brought his speed up to thirty miles an hour. As the rest joined him in his tour of the course, the caravan of cars slipped around the mocket[15] path,

---

[15] Terribly dirty.

getting themselves used to the road and the turns involved. This was an important part of the whole event. It was vital to feel how the road was driving that day. It was all very well if you'd driven it before but the weather in Scotland was unpredictable and there was no telling what state the road would be in on the day until you try it out.

The caravan drove down the track like a huge snake, crowds cheering them the whole way around. Agnus found it rather fun, not rushing, just driving around at a steady pace and feeling the road, if it could really be called a road. Agnus had seen single track farm roads up in the north-west that were in better condition than this. She was glad, beyond belief, that they had decided to upgrade the suspension and tyre size. Things would have been very uncomfortable otherwise.

As she went around, Agnus got more used to the conditions and started having fun with it. Her arches became smoother and she discovered that, when she relaxed her body, she was more likely to have a smoother run of it.

Round and round they went and when they came up to the finish line the crowd burst into an enormous roar of delight and refused to desist until the final car in the long caravan crossed the line, which, sadly, was being pushed.

When they had all crossed the line, they drove their cars to the pit stop area which had been specially created for the race. It was basically a patch of ground two hundred and fifty feet long and sixty feet wide. The first drivers to leave sat with their noses touching the longest edge of the area and the other two cars in the team parked up behind them. There was a makeshift road which led along the longest edge which worked its way up and joined the course, twenty-five feet before the starting line's position.

Here, they got out of the cars and congregated at the rear of the Charger which was the last to be taken out, discussing the course they had just gone around. Terry and Tommy both had things to tell her. The course was particularly muddy, this year, and some of the land had slipped onto the path. The organizers were constantly clearing the track of such things but you never knew if you'd hit something which they hadn't been able to catch yet. Careful and watchful driving was the key. "Don't take any chances," Tommy had said. "I don't give two hoots about the car but we don't want to lose you." He said it in a way that made Agnus wonder if that was a real possibility. It was dangerous, she knew, but she had never really thought that she wouldn't make it through to the other side, unless by 'the other side' you actually meant *the other side*.

It was a hard thought and she promised the boys that she'd be as careful as it were possible for her to be. As she turned to get something out of the car, Agnus got the fright of her life. There, standing right in front of her, was Connor O'Connell in the flesh.

"Hello there, darling," said Connor, grinning.

"I'm not your darling," humphed Agnus.

"Here, I just came here to wish you luck with the race," said Connor. "It can be dangerous out there," he smirked, "and I just want to be sure that you've got everything you require."

"We don't need anything from you," said Tommy, stomping up to the pair and moving Agnus behind him. "Why don't you just run off to Dopey, over there? A man must look after his family, in case he loses one, if you know what I mean. How is young Derik, by the by? Found him yet?"

The look that Connor gave Tommy was one that could etch steel. "I know where he is, yes," he said, slowly. "He'll be back home soon enough."

Agnus doubted that. Derik had been doing well with the Diagnostician and was happier than ever he had been. There was very little that could make him give all that up, now that he had found it, and, Agnus suspected, if Connor tried to use force, it may very well come down bad for him.

Agnus looked over to O'Connell's three cars, parked up along the line. They did look shiny but they were nothing to the glory of Misses Ford, Daphne *(Terry's Escort)* and Electra *(Tommy's Charger)*. She felt very special, standing next to her fancy Ford Escort. A great many people had been interested in it and that gave her a new sense of having just as much right to be there as anyone else.

That was something Agnus hadn't felt, up till that point. She knew that she was a pretty decent driver and the cars were tip-top but she hadn't previously felt like they would belong here, like the rest of them did. She thought they would be scorned at for trying this and expected to be the odd ones out. This was not the case. Agnus was delighted that people had given them such a nice welcome and the fact that these people were actually taking an interest in them and their cars, was uplifting and helped Agnus' nerves a lot.

As Agnus was contemplating all of this, there was the sound of another horn going off. At once, Connor turned his gaze to the three yellow Corsa's before turning his body in the same direction and tailing it away towards his son and the other two drivers in his team.

Chapter 38: The Race Begins

Agnus jumped into Misses Ford, clicked her belt into place and turned the key in the engine. Tommy stuck his head in through the window and said, "Just take it easy. I know it's the most laps done in the twenty-four hours that wins but remember, you don't have to do them all in the first four hours."

Agnus nodded in agreement and plugged her blue-rinsed perm into the tight helmet before making sure her face was clear of any stray strands. Nodding once more to Tommy and Terry in the rear view mirror as they watched her rev the engine a couple of time, she shifted into first gear, put some pressure on the accelerator and lifted her other foot carefully up off of the clutch. It would do their reputation no good at all if she were to stall the car before they even hit the course.

Agnus pulled out of her parking space and turned towards the track. This was it. This was the moment that she had been waiting for, ever since she had seen the magazine sitting on the kitchen table. The spark had been ignited then and now there were more than a few sparks inside the car she now drove.

She turned off of the access strip and took off onto the course.

Chapter 39: The Race

Agnus took it easy over the first few laps. There were twenty cars on the course and they were all jostling for a better position, except the guy in first place who was battling to keep it from falling into the hands of two Subaru's and a supped up original Mini Metro. The engine that the Mini team wished to use must have been larger than they could realistically fit in the space provided by the Mini's small frame because the one they chose was emerging out of the bonnet, top and centre. Extra exhausts had been installed on the bonnet as well and the gasses expelled were clearly visible as it flowed over the car.

As Agnus went around and around the course, again and again, over and over, she found her comfort zones and began to enjoy herself. She wasn't doing all that badly either. Running in tenth place, she was delighted. She didn't have any idea how she was going to fare against the rest of the teams but it was an amazing feeling to be right in the centre of things.

By the end of the first four hours of driving, Agnus was getting pretty tired and she was relieved when she was allowed to enter the pits and let Terry take over for a while. She had kept a steady tenth place through the first stage of the race and had even climbed to ninth just before entering the pit. Terry would build on that, she was sure.

As Agnus pulled into the pit, Terry shot out of it, like a bat out of Hell. He tore up the track and made Agnus' run look like a Sunday drive. He didn't simply turn at the corners, he drifted around them. He had been driving at this level for a long time and knew very well how to use the handbrake in his favour.

Lap by lap, he raced around the course, gaining places as he did. When it was time for him to come back in, he had already gained four places and they were now running in sixth.

He came tearing into the pit, almost as fast as he had left. Tommy, who had been sitting there revving his engine in preparation for Terry's re-entry, took off with a roar of the engine and the many, many horses he had under the bonnet went into overdrive. Tommy, the Charger's front wheels rising from the ground by a clear three feet and staying up for a good thirty yards before they bounced back down again, shifted into second gear. The front wheels re-joined the road with a bump and Terry rocketed out, leaving a cloud of dust in his wake.

Tommy hadn't been boasting when he had described the Charger to the girls. It was all that he had promised and more. It glided around the course like it had been built for it. The Charger's modified suspension was keeping up with the bad road and Tommy sped around like an Ambulance driver who wants to get home before his chips went cold. He overtook car after car, occasionally losing position but quickly gaining it again. When he came back into the pits after the twelfth hour, they were up in third place.

While Agnus was on her break, she slipped away from the course and took the opportunity to see how Liam and Charlie's team were doing and chat with them for a while. They had had a slow start but had gained a few placed after the fourth hour. They now sat in ninth place but were looking good for a better second stage.

Connor and his team were not doing as well. Their first car had popped a tyre on the tenth lap and driven straight into a tree. Although they too were well stocked up with new tyres, the smoke coming out of the engine would be more difficult to patch up. With only two cars left, Connor had still thought he was in with a chance but, as one of the remaining Corsas came back into the pit being towed by a rescue truck, his confidence dropped. The car had been hit from the rear by an out of control Vauxhall Astra. Both cars were shot and, as such, removed from the running.

Ruben, driving the only yellow Corsa left on the course, had a great deal of work ahead of him. There were still twelve hours to go and he had decided that it was likely that he would have to stop due to exhaustion at some point. He was, therefore, trying to get as many laps in as he could before he collapsed right there in the seat.

Agnus was living the dream, though, as she got back into her car and went around the course for her second run. Being in third place was amazing and she was keen to keep it that way. She gave it everything she had and did very well indeed. Not only did she manage to keep third place, she even overshot into second. With first place in her headlights, Agnus stepped up her game and almost came off of the track because of it. Unfortunately, it caused her to drop back into third and she ended up chasing it for the rest of her run time.

When she came in after her second run, Agnus was so tired that she had to go for a lie-down. It had been a wonderful experience and she would make sure that she was back there for Tommy taking the final four hours but, for now, she needed to shut her eyes and sleep.

Agnus retired to her camper van and dropped down on the bed as soon as she was through the door. Not even bothering to change, she drifted off, right there and then, her face buried in the soft pillows provided.

✯

When Agnus awoke it was to a start and Eva standing over her, shaking her awake.

"Wh… what is it?" Agnus asked.

"Come, quick," Eva said with a very serious tone of voice. "Terry's smashed his car and Tommy's had to take an early start. You need to be there for him coming back in or, *the Lord forbid*, if he crashes too."

Agnus jumped out of the bed and raced out the camper van and over to the pit stop area where Terry was sitting on the ground, Lilly holding a cloth up to his head.

"I'm telling you," Lilly was saying, "it needs stitches. We're going to have to get you to the medical tent."

"It's fine," said Terry. "I'll get it seen to after the race." He stood up when he saw Agnus coming and she saw the extent of the damage. Terry had a cut which ran from just above his temple, down past his ear and finishing a couple of centimetres from his jaw.

"Are you sure you shouldn't get that looked at?" asked Agnus, who was worried by the blood spilling down his face.

"I'll live," said Terry as he started to explain to her what had happened.

He had been doing very well at the start of his second run at the course but the trouble had come when he tried to overtake a Subaru and lost his grip on the road. He went into a spin and when he came to a stop, three other cars hit him from the side and that was the end of that. He had managed to get out of the car by his own efforts but the car itself was a total wreck and there was no way it was going to be able to continue.

As soon as Tommy heard that Terry was up and, if not walking then certainly staggering, about, he jumped into the Charger and took to the course with everything he had to give, shouting, "Get Agnus," out of the window as he sped off into the early hours of the day.

"And are you really not going to get that looked at?" Agnus asked, one last time.

Terry refused, point blank, and they transferred their view and concentration to Tommy who was ripping up the course like his life depended on it.

It was the nineteenth hour and there were only thirty-five minutes left before a new driver was to be inserted for the final four-hour stretch. It was a nerve-wracking time for everyone there. Lilly was being comforted by Big May as the young mum wept for fear of her husband's possible demise. She was absolutely distraught. Her face ran blue from the face paints.

Terry had barely escaped and had a long cut down his face that would soon become a life-long scar, if he ever got it sewn up. That and the fact that Tommy wasn't taking any prisoners out there made Lilly terrified of what might happen, should he make a mistake or if another car should bump him. At those speeds, if he got the slightest nudge in the wrong place, he'd be in the dirt before he knew it.

They watched as Tommy went around and around. The six big television screens that were positioned to face the bleachers gave them a very good view of the remaining cars. So far there had been thirteen crashes, seven sudden stalls and one who drove directly into the loch itself. That left thirty-nine cars still in play, twenty of which were on the course at that point.

The other nineteen drivers and their associated mechanics watched in terror of the next accident. By the grace of God, there had not been any fatalities so far. Terry wasn't the worst off by half but everyone was getting the care they needed (bar Terry) and they'd all be back on their feet soon enough, even if they did happen, *in one case*, to be an arm shorter than when he started. He had been rushed to the nearest hospital and the organisers later announced, in the fourteenth hour, that he was stable and shouting at the nurses to find him a television so that he could watch the rest of the race which was being televised by the STV network.

Five minutes before the end of the nineteenth hour, Agnus climbed into Misses Ford, patted her lovingly on the dashboard and said, softly, "Now, dear, this is it, the last stretch. One last run and we're there. Let's show them what we're made of, eh?" She turned the key and Misses Ford's engine roared into action.

"I had a wee play about with her, while you were out," said Lilly, explaining the more powerful sounding old Escort. "She should give you another few horses, at least.

Lily was right. As Agnus revved the engine, it was obvious that Misses Ford was ready for anything. She sounded like a lioness would, if you got too close to her cubs and she was telling you that this would be a good time to start backing up.

"Thanks," said Agnus. "That'll help, enormously."

"Just come back in safely," said Lilly, her voice riddled with nerves.

"You can't get rid of me that easily," Agnus replied, smiling as she put her foot down raced out of the pit, reaching a grand speed of fifty miles an hour before she fired herself out onto the course.

"I really hope she doesn't kill herself," said Lilly as she watched the disappearing Agnus. She then went over to her husband whose legs were shaking as he wobbled from the Charger and gave him a big hug, so strong that it knocked the wind out of him and he was left, in a bear-like grip, gasping for breath.

Even with their being one car down, they were still holding third place. Agnus gave the Escort a push and they flew around the course, overtaking all those who were out of the running and were only interested in making it to the twenty-four-hour mark without coming into collision with anything. You could tell who they were. As Agnus came up behind them they would move out of her way and allow her to pass, unchallenged.

The problems came when she came up to the two cars that were topping the list of laps completed, one of which was Ruben O'Connell, and they looked like they were going to take first and second place. They swerved and slowed in awkward spots; they brushed up against her when an overtaking manoeuvre was attempted; and they did everything else in their power to stop Agnus from taking the lead.

At present, all three of them were on the same number of laps for the day and, now in their final hour, it was going to be a tough battle between the three contenders for the trophy. Agnus pushed Misses Ford to the limit but, with all the swerving and bumping from the other two cars, Ruben's Corsa and a Subaru; she was finding it hard to keep her Escort on the course. Agnus remembered thinking, later, "Driving that wee Corsa, he shouldn't be so cocky."

However, whatever the O'Connells had done to that wee Corsa, it was enough to give Misses Ford a run for her money. If Agnus could just get past the irritating Irishman, she could leave him in her dust but Ruben must have realised this as well because she was having a really hard time getting into the right position.

The Subaru was still leading them but was still visible up ahead, only being around a second or two in front. Agnus tried again for another overtaking manoeuvre on the right-hand side and Ruben, again, moved to bash into the side of her. A sudden flash of memory popped into her head and she thought of something that Terry had said to her before the race.

She casually lifted her foot off of the accelerator, slowing down, and, as Ruben's back door met her bonnet,

Agnus swerved left, pushing Ruben's back end over. When Ruben was at ninety degrees to the road, Agnus fired down on the accelerator and pushed herself forward, knocking Ruben's back-end off course, leaving the poor Irishman facing in the wrong direction. When Agnus looked in her rearview mirror, she saw him beating the steering wheel with his fists, furiously.

Agnus looked forward again. The Subaru was just ahead of her and she found a new lease of life as she pressed further down on the accelerator, gaining speed as she also gained on the leading car. With the trophy within her grasp, Agnus went for it. She went around the track at speeds never seen before and the distance between the two cars lessened and lessened.

Before too long, Agnus had gained on the Subaru enough to consider passing it. The Subaru was not having any of it, though. She swerved and slid, left and right, making sure there was no way for Agnus to pass.

As it came to the point when they were three minutes from the end of the race, Agnus thought she was done and that the Subaru was going to take first place. Then she remembered something else. There was one thing that she hadn't tried. When Tommy had last finished working on Misses Ford, he had said that he'd incorporated a wee secret. Agnus had asked why it was a secret. Tommy explained that, although it wasn't very good form, the use of NOS was not on the list of banned items.

Agnus didn't have a clue what NOS was and told him so. Apparently, it was short for Nitrous Oxide. If you use it, it can give you a sudden and powerful boost of speed.

This was exactly what Agnus needed now. She looked down at the steering wheel and found the button she would need to press. She hovered her thumb over it, found a gap and went for it. When she was pointing the right way and had spun her wheels straight, Agnus held on tight and pressed the button.

She shot past the Subaru at a speed unimagined by either of the drivers. Agnus held up a hand to wave at the other driver and they did to her exactly the same thing as she had done to Ruben. This time, however, Misses Ford went into a spin. The only compensation was that she was at least moving in the right direction, blocking all attempts to overtake.

Agnus' heart leaped when, just as she was slowing down, the final horn went off, announcing the end of the twenty-four hours and a new champion. Coming to a standstill, she let out a deep breath of relief and dropped her head onto the steering wheel. It was done.

Chapter 40: The Finish Line

Agnus was in a daze when she came around. She was still strapped into the car which told her nothing. She felt around her body and found that she seemed to be all in one piece. There were a few bumps and she would have a bruise on her forehead for some time to come but, all things considered, she was doing alright.

Agnus looked around at the muddy track going each way and saw, through blurred eyes, Eva, Lilly, Big May, Tommy and Terry all running towards her as fast as their legs would carry them. Agnus, however, managed to get her door open, after a couple of kicks, and pulled herself out of the knackered vehicle. As she staggered forward, the last thing she saw before she blacked out again and hit the mud, face first, was Lilly screaming at her to stop moving.

The rest of the day was a complete blur. She remembered being at each point, in turn, but getting to and from them was a complete mystery. There was the point where all her friends lifted her up into the air, celebrating their impressive win; there was the point where she was standing on the highest podium, receiving her medal with Tommy and Terry; there was the point when she finally managed to have a rest, back in her camper van; and there was the point when she blanked out for the fifth and final time, that day.

Chapter 41: The Celebrations

A few days later, when Agnus and Terry had healed and Tommy had rested, the gang all got together for a proper dinner in a very fancy restaurant, paid for out of the fifty-thousand-pound cash prize that the girls had never realised they were fighting for. Big May, a perfect mathematician when she needed to be, quickly figured out that it would be eight thousand, three hundred and thirty-three pounds each, with a pound to put in the charity box. The girls' minds, instantly and in unison, went and planned a holiday somewhere in the sun.

The dinner was fabulous and the girls all felt very important as they ate in the expensive restaurant, in their finest clothing. The trophy sat at the end of the table and, every time they looked at it, they were filled with a warm delight, in awe that they actually won. That had never been expected and they were all dizzy with excitement, disbelief and champagne.

They talked all night, even until they were the only ones left, laughing and joking in their own corner of the room. They discussed everything that they had done since the beginning of their quest and they all agreed that it had been a quest. There was no better word for it. They had found their goal, headed after it, conquered it and came home in time for dinner and medals. That was the very definition of a quest and Agnus had loved every minute of it.

Well, maybe not every minute but she had certainly had a great time building and racing that small car in a real rally. The fact that she got to do it with her three best friends was the icing on the cake. On her next project, she would definitely have them on board. She didn't, however, tell the other three girls that she would be planning something bigger and better for them to attempt. She thought it best to bask in their glory for now and enjoy their win.

They all had an amazing time filled with joy and laughter and, when they were eventually asked to vacate, so the staff could go home, they did so, singing, "Loch Lomond" at the top of their voices. They were stopped a couple of times, by two separate pairs of police officers, as they waddled and staggered through the city streets[16] on their way home. Each time they held up the cup for the officers to see, screaming, "We won!" very loudly.

Thankfully, on both occasions, the police went easy on them and they were allowed to move along with only a caution to keep the noise down. When they got to a crossroads, Agnus, Charlie and Liam went one way; Lilly, Big May, Tommy and Terry went another way; and Eva and her husband went straight ahead. Big hugs were passed all around before the group split up and a lot of joyful tears were spilt.

When Agnus, Charlie and Liam arrived back at the house, Liam went straight up to his room. He had been secretly half-inching[17] drinks from the rest of the group all night and was a little worse for wear. Agnus and Charlie were fully aware of this and decided to make it a life lesson. A greasy fry-up would be produced in the morning, for his aromatic pleasure.

Agnus and Charlie stayed up for a while in order to watch Agnus' show together. Their relationship was stronger than ever it was and they were both going to make sure it stayed that way. They had had their moment, back there, but after explanations and recriminations, they were back on a sure footing and Agnus didn't want it to end.

From now on, they would be doing a lot more things together and that started at home. It started with, 'The Chase'. Charlie got more questions correct than Agnus did but she

---
[16] That being the ladies and their husbands who were staggering, not the police.
[17] Cockney Rhyming Slang: '*half-inching*'=*pinching*; to thieve.

decided to forgive him this once and let him have this short-lived victory. Agnus glanced at him. He really was the best thing that had happened to her, not counting Liam, and she loved the man with a passion.

As they sat and watched Bradley giggle his way through the questions, Agnus delighted in the weekend. She had her excitement in the race; they had had a wonderful celebration; and she had her wonderful son and husband. Basically, she had everything that her heart desired and she wanted this day to never end.

Agnus went to bed, that night, in a state of pure happiness and joy over a job well done. She almost wished she could do it all again.

Chapter 42: The Broken Cup

Agnus awoke with a smile on her face. She was still stiff but there was no sign of the expected hangover. She lay there for a while, enjoying the new sun on her face. It was a glorious day outside, from what she could tell, and the warmth was very relaxing. She cast her mind back to the events of the last couple of months. It was strange, although she could remember it all, there was a slight dullness to the memories, almost as if they were slipping away.

Agnus heart dropped slightly, at the thought of this. Was this the start of it? Was this where her memory started to fade and her body break? The thought was a sad one but not unexpected. She hadn't exactly taken very good care of herself over the last while and it was bound to bring unwanted consequences.

Her alarm went off and, eyes still closed and wondering who would have set it, she reached over quickly to hit the snooze button. As she did, her hand hit something, knocking it to the floor. Agnus forced herself to roll over properly and peered down over the mattress to the object lying on the floor.

When she focused on the object in question, it filled her with confused thoughts. Before her, or rather below her, lying on the carpet was her favourite green mug. It was in one piece and had the trickling remains of tea flowing slowly out.

Agnus stayed still for a while, unsure of how to explain this. She eventually reached down and picked it up to see if someone had found it and glued it back together. If they had, it was an incredible job. There were no signs of cracks and definitely no chips or missing pieces. It looked just like it did before she smashed it. She tried to remember when that was and found that that particular memory was also starting to fade.

Pulling herself together, Agnus got herself up out of bed and made her way through the hall to the bathroom. She washed and brushed her teeth before wandering downstairs to the sittingroom. It was odd. She couldn't figure out what but there was definitely something wrong with the picture.

Agnus gave the place a quick tidy, getting a case of Deja Vu as she did. It was very strange. The world didn't feel right and she couldn't, for the life of her, define why.

Agnus took the rubbish she had collected and carried it through to the kitchen, dropping it in the trash. She went to make herself a cup of tea only to find that the tea jar was empty. Going to the cupboard to get some more from out of the box, Agnus found, to her astonishment, that someone had put all her stuff back into the cupboards which they had been in before she had her clear out and had changed everything around.

Who would do that? Agnus wondered, staring at the cupboards, one by one as if they were going to be any help in the matter. She was getting a strange feeling about today, getting real feelings of having had this day before. Somebody, somewhere, must be playing a sick joke on her.

Agnus made her tea, regardless and went through to watch her show. She was angered to the limit when she discovered that all the unwatched episodes were missing from the drive and the only ones that were left were from months ago, two months, to be exact.

Agnus thought about this and then shook herself. *No*, she said, shaking a thought from her mind, someone was doing all this to her and when she got a hold of the trickster she would beat them six ways to Sunday.

She flicked the channels until she found a repeated episode and started to watch that. She wondered, for the briefest of seconds before she expelled the idea, where Sergey and Tarquin were. This was the time, when she was getting stressed, that they normally chose to make an appearance but, as yet, they were not planning on showing up. *Maybe I'm just rid of them for good, now,* she had thought with a hopeful smile.

Agnus enjoyed her show, in the peace and quiet of her home. It occurred to her that she hadn't seen Charlie or Liam so far. She presumed that Liam was, most likely, still in his bed and that Charlie had popped out for some breakfast rolls or something similar.

Once her show had finished, Agnus switched off the television and wandered through to the kitchen again to wash her mug. She still couldn't fathom how it was mysteriously back together again after being smashed. As she stood at the sink, rinsing the mug under the tap, she realised one thing she had seen when coming through and had only just processed.

Agnus turned slowly. Looking down at the kitchen table, she saw something that made her heart stop. Sitting there, in exactly the same place it had been when first she saw it, was the racing magazine which had originally given her the inspiration for her whole project. Her legs started to shake as her mind started to piece things together. The unbroken mug; the cupboards; the television show being absent from the DVR; and state of the sittingroom when first she had come downstairs.

"Surely not," said Agnus, as she worked all this through her tired brain. She looked around for a newspaper and, when she failed to find one, she rushed through to the sittingroom again, switched on the television again and pressed the red button.

Agnus couldn't believe it. She really couldn't. The date on the screen was two months behind. Was it really possible? Could it really all have been one long dream? Her mind was overwhelmed by the thought. If it were true, then nothing in the last two months ever happened. Agnus tried to wrap her head around it and found it very difficult.

She cast her mind back over the ever-fading memories of their glorious eight-week race to the finishing horn. The memories slipped away from her, one by one, and it became ever more difficult to retrieve them.

As she stood there, still holding the remote control, she had a sudden thought. If this were two months ago then Charlie and Liam would be outside working on their car for the race. "It's not," she kept telling herself. "Charlie's out at the shops and Liam is in his bed. There's nothing to worry yourself about."

Just in order to put her mind at rest, Agnus crossed the sittingroom and opened the front door. She walked, just as slowly, around the house and out to the garage where the boys had been storing their car.

She was met with something only half-expected. The garage door was wide open and there was a car up on two jacks... Charlie and Liam's car. She walked up to the garage and looked at the vehicle and then gave Charlie, who was lying under the vehicle, a short sharp kick. He immediately slid out from under the car and stood up.

"Come out to see what we're up to, are you?" he asked.

"Why are you taking it apart again?" Agnus asked, guessing at the answer. "The race is all over."

"We're not," replied a confused Charlie, "we're still rebuilding it," he put his hand on her shoulder, "the race isn't for a couple of months yet."

The truth of it all came bubbling up inside her and she started to see the world for what it was. She had dreamed the whole thing. It was, by all means, a vivid dream but a dream all the same.

She thought about it for a minute, getting everything into perspective before looking up at Charlie and saying, "Charlie, dear. There's something I need to do. It's a bit dangerous, I know, but I have a feeling it'll all work out in the end."

-THE END-

Printed in Great Britain
by Amazon